CRAVE

CHARITY PARKERSON

--Warning: This book is intended for readers over the age of 18.

Copyright © 2017 Charity Parkerson
Editor: Hercules Editing and Consultants
Photographer: RLS Images | Randy Sewell
Cover model: Cody Criswell
All rights reserved.

INTRODUCTION

LIRE IS A DEMON. AN ADDICTION. A CURSE. DOUGAL'S ONLY HOPE.

Now that the Hellish clan has their first real lead on the whereabouts of the demon pack they've been hunting, they're off to New Orleans, minus one —Dougal.

When Dougal traded his life for Jonathan's, he had no idea what he'd done. He'd expected the demon, Lire, would kill him—not keep him as a toy. With his mind a mess and no hope in sight, Dougal's completely at Lire's mercy. Luckily, Lire has one weak spot, and his name is Jonathan.

In this third installment of Hellish, Jonathan's attention is split between helping Dougal find a way to survive the damage he suffered as Lire's prisoner and saving the world from whatever the demons have planned for the humans. With Mammon, the fifth prince of hell running loose, things aren't looking great.

With the help of new friends and old, Hellish might have a shot at stopping Mammon from unleashing his evil on the world. Then again, sometimes greed wins the day.

1

The Hellish clan had been fighting demons for as long as Dougal could remember. They rushed in anytime a pack grew out of control, threatening the exposure of their world. His clan was the line between good and evil. If they sat back and did nothing, there'd be nothing left of the world humans knew. Demons were the equivalent of a zombie apocalypse. They'd multiply and spread out of control, possessing the bodies and killing the souls of every available human they could find until there was nothing but rotting meat left behind. Demons served no purpose beyond spreading evil.

The irony wasn't lost on Dougal that he now depended on the very thing he'd sworn to destroy to feed the sickness growing inside him. The cramping in Dougal's stomach got worse every day. Neither blood nor food eased him. Dougal stared at his reflection in the bathroom mirror of the home he now shared with his captor. He looked the same. Even with the steam from his shower distorting the image of his nude body, Dougal could tell—physically—being with Lire hadn't changed him. It was his insides that were a mess. The temptation to claw at his skin like the worst sort of drug addict was a real thing living inside him. He shook to the point of giving himself motion sickness. Dougal worried he'd develop some sort of fucked up eye tick at any second. He couldn't remember the last time he'd fed. Every time Lire touched him, Dougal's fangs grew. He wanted to sink them into Lire's neck and draw the demon's acidic blood inside him. Dougal didn't care it would probably kill him. There was no sense or logic to his current circumstances. This wasn't a love affair. Dougal hadn't moved to New Orleans and shacked up with a demon because he couldn't resist the man's charms. Except Dougal couldn't resist Lire.

He'd known trading his life for his prince's life wouldn't mean happy days were ahead. Dougal had thought it would mean his death. Not this. Never this. Lire didn't keep him prisoner. Dougal was free to dissipate at any time and go back to his clan. Except Dougal would never be free again and it had nothing to do with having given his word. His word *was* everything, but Dougal couldn't stare at his reflection and lie to himself. Lire was a lilin demon. No one—

human or otherwise—could endure Lire's touch as many times or as often as Dougal had without becoming half insane with the need to have it every second of every day. That was what sex demons did. They fed and fed from their victims until there was nothing left of the person's mind.

Dougal swallowed. Sandpaper lived in his throat. No matter how much he drank, the thirst never left. He knew he needed to feed. Lire had tried forcing him. He'd brought women in from the streets, demanding Dougal take their blood. No men had been offered. Lire had made no secret Dougal would die if he touched another of those. He belonged to Lire now. No matter how many humans Lire dragged before Dougal, Dougal couldn't do it. The only heartbeat he heard was Lire's. The only blood he smelled was from the demon who owned him. Even its corrosion didn't deter Dougal from his need to taste it. He was sick. Like a pica-stricken human craving the taste of bleach, he needed Lire's blood in his mouth.

When Lire's image appeared in the mirror at Dougal's back, Dougal wondered for a moment if his mind had finally snapped. It was like his gut-wrenching cravings had conjured Lire from thin air. He clung to the edge of the bathroom counter, scared to move or breathe. Dougal was a junkie—frightened his dealer wouldn't put out.

"So lovely," Lire said, brushing his fingers down

Dougal's spine. The sound of Lire's voice hardened Dougal's cock. His eyelids weighed a ton, falling closed beneath Lire's touch. It didn't last long. He couldn't stand not being able to see Lire. The man's brown hair hung over one shoulder and called for Dougal's fingers to brush it aside. But it was Lire's sexy eyes that always captured and held Dougal's focus. They were copper with a hint of unnatural light. Dougal's gaze latched on to the reflection of them in the mirror. Lire stared back every bit as intently. As he looked on, the demon's eyes turned amethyst.

Lire took a step forward. His chest collided with Dougal's back. Even with Lire wearing a shirt, Dougal could feel the press of the man's nipple piercing against his skin. His dick leaked. Pre-cum rolled down his length. Despite his over-parched state, saliva filled Dougal's mouth. Lire's skin was like fire, scorching Dougal.

"I can smell your lust," Lire said, kissing Dougal's shoulder. "Tell me all your dirty fantasies. I can give you anything."

He could. Dougal would know. There was nothing Lire hadn't done to Dougal's body in the past few months. Dougal had begged for all of it. He didn't doubt for a moment that he would plead for Lire's touch again today.

"You're wearing my favorite outfit," Lire said as his hands smoothed down Dougal's bare sides and came to rest on his hips. With every word Lire spoke, he let his lips lightly brush Dougal's skin. Dougal didn't doubt the move was contrived. The goosebumps on Dougal's skin didn't give a fuck how practiced Lire's moves were. "It's almost like you were standing here waiting for me."

Perhaps he had been. Dougal no longer knew. Lire's hands on his body ruled his mind. "Please?" There it was. Dougal didn't care. The desperate note to his voice didn't faze Dougal at all. He needed Lire.

Lire palmed Dougal's cock and stroked. Dougal's knees weakened. "A man can't live by sex alone," Lire said, pulling away and making Dougal cry out in denial. "Shhh," Lire soothed. "I'll take care of you. Have I ever made you suffer?" Dougal didn't answer. He was suffering now. Every second of every day had been torture since the day Lire came into his life. "Do this one thing for me, and I'll make you fly." Dougal let Lire lead him from the bathroom to the bedroom, because he had no other choice. Wherever Lire went, Dougal would follow. A girl around nineteen sat on the edge of their bed. Dougal stumbled when he caught sight of her. She looked young and fragile. Her features were soft—almost like porcelain. Dougal was reminded of a doll he'd once seen. They had the same red hair and delicate features. The woman stared calmly at the corner of the room. Dougal didn't doubt she was under Lire's spell and wouldn't remember this moment—the one where he didn't touch her.

Lire held Dougal's hands and stare as he walked backward, moving toward the girl. "You need blood."

Dougal's stomach cramped at the idea. His fangs were cutting into his bottom lip from having Lire's hands on his body. He knew Lire was right. Each step became harder than the last. Lire's woodsy scent filled Dougal's nostrils. His dick throbbed, screaming for Lire's touch. An image of sinking his fangs into Lire's femoral artery flared to life inside Dougal's mind. In his head, Lire's blood tasted every bit as delicious as the man's dick. There was no burning or poison.

Lire's eyes switched from amethyst back to copper. "Just one drink," he cajoled. "One little taste and then I'll be free to make you come. You'll chant my name."

He knew Lire was right. Not only did Dougal need blood if he wanted to survive, he would scream Lire's name. Without a word, he moved to stand between the girl's knees. He dropped his chin to his chest and stared down at her. A lead weight landed on Dougal's chest. Everything was wrong. This was wrong. He was nude. His hard dick was inches from this girl he didn't want. Each breath Dougal took came harder than the last. He tried focusing on her heartbeat—on his hunger. Nothing happened. The only sound penetrating the blood rushing through his ears was the sound of his own rapid breathing.

"Just one sip," Lire said behind him.

Dougal closed his eyes and tried harder to focus. He needed this girl's blood. He would eventually die without it. Lire would ease the ache if he did this. Dougal bent, hoping to catch a whiff of the blood rushing through her veins. His stomach heaved. Bile rose in his throat. Dougal swallowed. The room spun. He couldn't do this. His stomach heaved again. Dougal squeezed eyes shut even harder, hoping his head would stop spinning, and the world disappeared.

2

---

onathan relaxed in his cocoon of arms and legs. His men breathed deep, setting the perfect tone to lull Jonathan into dreamland, but his mind raced. Ever since they'd moved to New Orleans, Jonathan couldn't shake the voice in the back of his mind, whispering they were close. They stood on the precipice of something huge. Jonathan just didn't know what. To keep from going insane, he researched. He read every myth and lore about the area, and there was a lot. New Orleans was a hot bed of supernatural phenomena. Unfortunately, there was no way to tell what was truth and what business owners had created to sell bullshit items to tourists. Of course, Jonathan also couldn't pretend he didn't need to keep his mind busy for other reasons as well. Learning he was Celeste's great-grandson was a huge pill to swallow. He hadn't even known who Celeste was until days before learning of his ties to her. Now, here he was—a Nephilim. He'd had to Google that too.

Several times he'd wondered if his connection to Celeste was the reason he'd trusted the demon, Lire, for no other reason than his gut had told him to. As the seventh son of a seventh son, even an evil father couldn't squelch the blessings of Lire's birth. Plus, Lire had chosen Celeste's side. He fought against his dark nature at every turn. That didn't mean they'd seen Dougal once Lire had claimed the warrior as his. Once Dougal had traded his life for Jonathan's, Lire had swept Dougal away. The guilt was massive.

"What are you doing?" Cin's tired-sounding whisper pulled at the corners of Jonathan's mouth. He couldn't help but smile when his men were around.

"Research," Jonathan whispered back. "I didn't mean to wake you."

"What are you researching?" Cin's hand slipped up Jonathan's inner thigh as he asked the question, distracting Jonathan.

For a moment, Jonathan scrambled to recall their topic. "Um, the area, I guess. I'm looking at local lore and whatnot."

Cin came up onto his elbow and eyed the screen of Jonathan's laptop. "What do you want to know? I probably lived through most of it."

He hadn't thought of that. "Everything," Jonathan answered honestly. "Do your people have their own set of history books? Because that would make my life so much easier."

Cin scratched his chin. Damn, everything about the man from his soft hair to his blue eyes aroused Jonathan's senses. "My people are your people too now, but yeah, we do. They're kept safe by appointed guardians. The only set I've ever seen personally are back in Scotland. I imagine there is an American version, but this area hasn't had a king since the early 1800s when its last one was burned alive by religious zealots. So I wouldn't know who to ask about their whereabouts."

Jonathan was fascinated. "There's more than one king?"

Cin nodded. "Sure. Niall's father rules Scotland, England, and Wales. The rest of the world is similarly divided. Canada, the US, and Mexico is another section carved off for one ruler. Being without a king has made this area a bit like the Wild West for supernatural beings."

"I have so much to learn—"

"You should ask Faolan," Niall said, cutting Jonathan off and proving he'd been awake and listening. "He's a history buff."

Jonathan switched his attention Niall's way. His dark hair stood in every direction, looking like he'd been tossing and turning all night rather than sleeping soundly as he had. Jonathan's palms itched to run his fingers through the man's soft locks. "I'm sorry. No one's getting any sleep because of me."

Niall shifted onto his knees and snagged Jonathan's laptop. After setting it aside, he forced Jonathan onto his back before scooching over until he had Jonathan squished between Cin and him. "Never apologize for giving me a reason to hold my sexy men, but you can't keep staying up to sift through whatever it is you're finding on the internet. You need sleep."

"And more than half the stuff you find online isn't true," Cin said, adding his opinion on the matter.

"I—" A massive weight landed on Jonathan, cutting him off and forcing the air from his lungs. Unnatural light gray eyes focused on him from inches away. His men shouted. Jonathan didn't have enough oxygen left to draw a big enough breath to protest.

"I'm calling in a favor." Lire's words were the only warning Jonathan got before the world spun so fast he couldn't breathe. A sharp pain stabbed him in the brain. Everything went dark around the edges. For a moment, Jonathan wondered if his head would explode. As quickly as it happened, it was over. Jonathan stood in the center of an unfamiliar bedroom. Dougal was sprawled spread eagle across the top of a massive bed. He was nude. Jonathan wanted to look away, but there wasn't much else to focus upon.

He chose to hold Lire's stare. The demon looked panicked. That fact stopped Jonathan's protests over being abducted before they ever left his lips. "Help him."

Jonathan's gaze slid Dougal's way once more. Against his will, he dropped his chin and focused on his own less than dressed state. Lire growled. A black pair of workout shorts appeared on Jonathan's skin, hiding his nudity. Jonathan's mind was a mess. He was having a hard time gripping reality. Only moments earlier, he'd been squashed between his men. Now, he was inside Lire's lair with no clue how he'd come to be there. He cleared his throat, trying to come to terms.

"What's wrong?"

Lire shoved him toward Dougal. "He's been refusing to feed. I think he's dying."

The alarm in Lire's voice got Jonathan moving. Without another thought, he scrambled onto the bed with Dougal. This man had traded his life for Jonathan's. He couldn't let Dougal down. The huge vamp's skin was like ice to the touch. Jonathan patted his cheek, trying to wake him. A slice of dark blue eyes peeked out at him. Jonathan wasn't sure if Dougal was lucid. His heartbeat was weak—like he was barely hanging on.

"Do you know who I am?" Jonathan asked, trying to get a grasp on how bad things were.

"My king," Dougal whispered, sounding as if he'd

been existing on a diet of nails since he'd disappeared with Lire.

"Close enough," Jonathan said, lifting Dougal's head and pressing the man's face against the crook of his neck. "Take my blood."

"Can't," Dougal whispered against Jonathan's skin.

Terror choked Jonathan. He could feel Dougal slipping further away by the second. Jonathan dug deep for courage and hardened his voice. "I'm ordering you to take my blood." He had no idea if Dougal would obey. Since mating with the prince, Jonathan hadn't tried taking any sort of control of the clan. They were his friends, not his slaves.

Tell me where you are. Niall's panicked demand rang out loudly inside Jonathan's head as Dougal's fangs pierced his vein.

I'm fine. It's fine. Jonathan kept his thoughts calm for anyone listening. He knew Cin and Niall would hear, but he wasn't sure if Dougal could hear his thoughts while taking his blood. Jonathan never drank from anyone other than his mates. He had no reference point here. *Dougal needs me, but everything is okay.*

I'll fucking kill Lire. Niall's thoughts weren't reassuring Jonathan.

We owe him this. Jonathan hoped his reminder would calm Niall. *Plus, I'm here for Dougal. I'll explain later. Just breathe.* Jonathan wasn't sure if that last part had been for his mates or himself. He wasn't used to having anyone's mouth on his skin other than Niall's and Cin's. It wasn't uncomfortable or sexual in the least. That part surprised him. Each and every time one of his men took his blood, it came with a happy ending. He was getting light-headed. Dougal was taking too much, but Jonathan didn't know how to stop it without risking ripping open his throat by pushing Dougal away.

He gently pressed his hands against Dougal's chest. "Don't kill me, okay?" Jonathan whispered, hoping not to spook him. Dougal seemed a bit out of his head and Jonathan wasn't sure what to expect. The huge vamp didn't pull away right away. Jonathan swayed. Dougal jerked back, pressing into the bed as if trying to get as far away from Jonathan as possible. Jonathan tried moving away. It didn't happen. Dougal's chest came rushing up to meet him as Jonathan fell forward.

"Holy shit." Jonathan tried breathing through his nose. His limbs felt heavy.

"Shit," Lire spat, sounding more pissed off than Jonathan had ever heard him. He sought the demon with his gaze. Instead of finding Lire, Jonathan spotted a red-haired girl sitting on the end of the bed. He hadn't noticed her before.

"Lire." Even to his own ears, Jonathan's voice sounded slurred and weak.

"I'm here," Lire said, tugging at him and pulling Jonathan into a sitting position.

"Why do you have a girl sitting on your bed?"

"It's a damn good thing I do," Lire said instead of answering. "You need her blood."

In spite of his weakened state and thirst, Jonathan winced. He hated the idea of sinking his fangs into anyone other than one of his mates. "No, thank you. Send me home and Niall or Cin will take care of me."

Lire snapped his fingers, and the girl moved to the edge of the bed next to Jonathan. "Drink. You're not going home just yet."

Jonathan was so tired. He wanted to rage against Lire's claim but didn't have the energy. "Fuck," he grumbled as he scooched closer to the woman who was there only in body. Even from the very first time he'd drunk anyone's blood, Jonathan had never been disgusted over the matter. It had been Cin and Niall beneath his fangs. This was gross. He didn't want to do it. Jonathan pushed the woman aside with the last of his strength. He fell backward, sprawling across Dougal's chest again. "I need Niall."

"Goddamn it," Lire growled. "What the fuck is wrong with both of you? Even on the verge of death, you're fucking picky. What sort of bullshit is that?"

Lire's anger was evident. Despite his exhaustion, Jonathan's interest was piqued. His clan had kept Lire prisoner for months and Jonathan hadn't once seen Lire lose his temper. Now, Lire was furious. Jonathan could only watch with a detached sort of interest.

Lire glanced at his feet and put his hands on his hips before straightening again. With a snap of his fingers, the woman disappeared.

"Did you just kill an innocent woman?" Jonathan was hitting the loopy stage. He fought the urge to laugh even though it wasn't funny.

"For fuck's sake," Lire said, not answering Jonathan's question. "I'll bring your blue-eyed beauty but not your prince."

The chuckle he'd been suppressing sneaked out. "In spite of our unique relationship dynamics, Cin is the jealous one, and as much as he cares for his clansman, he won't understand me being in bed with a naked Dougal."

"Cin?"

Shit. Jonathan was out of his head. He hadn't realized he'd been handing a demon his mates' names. Names were power. "Never mind," Jonathan grumbled. Jonathan closed his eyes and gathered his strength.

I need you. Follow my voice.

"What the fuck?" Lire said, jumping out of the way as Niall appeared at the edge of the bed. He eyed Niall. "How did you do that? This house is warded against vampires. You shouldn't be able to breach my wards without me leading you inside."

Niall didn't bother sparing a glance for Lire. "I didn't do it. Jonathan did." Without a word, he climbed into the bed and offered his vein to

Jonathan. An inner sigh of relief poured through Jonathan as Niall's blood filled his mouth. He intentionally didn't take enough to satisfy him. Jonathan wouldn't weaken Niall. It was a true testament to how close he was to death that his body didn't stir while drinking from his mate. The instant Jonathan was taken care of, Niall turned his fury on Lire. A silver knife appeared in his hand and against Lire's throat too fast to anticipate it. "If you ever pull that shit again, putting my mate's life in danger, I'll—"

"What?" Lire said, interrupting Niall and taunting him. Jonathan didn't like Lire's tone or the direction things were headed. "Without me, your mate would be dead."

"As much as I love watching alpha men swing their dicks around, I think I'm gonna pass out soon if I don't get some more blood. I imagine Dougal would say the same if he wasn't already out cold."

Niall released a litany of curse words, impressing Jonathan. "Since I can't zap you back home, the same way this douche zapped you here, I'll give Dougal my blood."

A loud growl—like an angry wolf's—reverberated off the walls. It took Jonathan a second to realize the sound came from Lire. Lire bared his teeth at Niall. "You'll not touch him."

"Then take Jonathan home," Niall said, not

hesitating to go nose to nose with Lire no matter how enraged the demon seemed to be.

"No. He's still needed."

Jonathan was so tired. He wasn't sure if he cared. After rolling to his side and cuddling up to Dougal, Jonathan let out a loud sigh. "It's okay. Dougal's so warm. I'll sleep while you figure it out." Jonathan rubbed his cheek against Dougal's chest. Without warning, Dougal's swirling emotions invaded Jonathan's brain. He cringed against the sudden onslaught. "Oh no," Jonathan cooed. "It's so dark inside his head. This seems familiar. Where have I seen this before?" Jonathan asked more for himself than anyone. He pressed his ear to Dougal's chest, listening to the vamp's heartbeat. Jonathan hadn't felt this drunk since the night he'd turned twenty-one and he'd almost died from alcohol poisoning. "Poor Lire," Jonathan mused aloud. "You're always breaking your toys."

"I'll get Cin," Niall said, sounding almost sad. "Don't close your thoughts to me, baby," Niall added, reminding Jonathan he wouldn't be able to return if he didn't lead Niall back.

Jonathan nodded. His face squished against Dougal's chest with each motion. When Niall disappeared, Jonathan reached for Lire's hand. He'd done so without thought and was more than a little surprised when Lire accepted. Their palms met. Jonathan had forgotten how hot Lire's touch was. He dragged Lire closer, ignoring the man's closed features. The demon couldn't hide anything from Jonathan.

Jonathan flattened Lire's hand to Dougal's chest and held it there. "If you love him as the warrior you first met, you'll have to heal the damage you've done to his mind."

Lire's expression never changed. "I'm a demon. I love nothing."

Since Jonathan was too tired to argue, and it didn't matter if Lire admitted what Jonathan could see in his mind, he shrugged. "Heal him anyway."

"My powers don't work that way," Lire argued, but he didn't pull away.

A smile pulled at the corners of Jonathan's mouth. "Sure they do, seventh son of a seventh son. You healed me when I was dying. It's Dougal's turn."

Cin and Niall appeared at the edge of the bed. They both wore only jeans and looked so fucking delicious. Jonathan wondered how he'd been in bed with both men only minutes earlier and had been using his time for research. He wouldn't make that mistake again once they got back home.

"Fuck me," Cin growled as he pushed Lire out of the way and scrambled onto the bed. "Niall hadn't been lying. You're a fucked up mess, baby. You need to take my blood." Jonathan tried sitting up, but nothing happened. Cin smiled. "It's okay. I'll come to you," Cin said as he pulled Jonathan off Dougal before straddling his hips and leaning down so Jonathan could sink his fangs into his neck.

The instant Cin's blood filled his mouth, Cin's voice filled his head. *Why are you in bed with a nude Dougal?*

I was helping. Looks like I'm not finished yet.

A loud sigh rang through Jonathan's mind and it wasn't his. *At least the beast clothed you before forcing you to give away all your blood.*

He needs more. Niall and you will have to stock up. I have a feeling I'll need you again tonight. Jonathan licked Cin's neck, sealing the puncture marks with a little more enthusiasm than necessary. He loved the way Cin tasted. *Plus, you'll need your strength.*

Evil man. "On it," Cin said aloud before focusing on Niall. "We need to find somewhere else to feed. We need to stock up." He switched his gaze to Lire. "The fact that you once saved my mate is the only reason I'm sparing your life. That, and you're doing this for my clansman."

"He wouldn't be in this position if not for you, though," Niall grumbled.

Jonathan was feeling stronger. His head didn't spin as much. He rolled onto his knees and tried again to wake Dougal, but his words were for his mates. "Stop it. This isn't helping anything. He could've let Dougal die." Jonathan glanced over his shoulder. "Dougal did this to himself. Any other demon would've let him starve. Celeste trusts Lire and so do I."

With a curse in a foreign language, Cin and Niall disappeared.

Dougal's eyes finally peeked open. "My king," Dougal said, sounding drowsy.

"Still close enough," Jonathan said, trying to keep Dougal awake. "You need to take more of my blood."

"Is that why you're here?"

"Sheesh, you're in rough shape," Jonathan muttered. He held his wrist over Dougal's mouth. "Take my blood, babe. Niall and Cin are getting more for me." While holding his gaze, Dougal gently bit down on his wrist. Jonathan's head spun. Dougal tried pulling away. With a pat on the man's chest, Jonathan settled him back down. "Nope. Don't worry over me. I'll be fine. Take what you need." The second Dougal licked the wound closed, Jonathan found himself using Dougal's chest as his pillow once more. He felt like shit all the way to his bones. Still, he couldn't give up on Lire. He held out his hand for Lire once more, half expecting Lire wouldn't accept. To his surprise, the demon rushed to hold his hand again.

Jonathan flattened the man's hand to Lire's chest once more. "It's easy," Jonathan assured him. "However you healed me, heal your man the same way. Close your eyes, reach inside, and see his sickness. Then, take it away." Jonathan moved over, giving Lire room to work. He was too tired to watch the show. Instead, he closed his eyes and snuggled deeper into the bed.

"I didn't heal you. Celeste did."

Jonathan wasn't listening. His brain wouldn't work right. Lire had a damn comfy mattress for a demon. Decadence in all things, he guessed. Damn, he was cold. Lire needed to turn up the heat if he expected Jonathan to give away all his blood. A soothing warmth overcame him—like the breeze coming off the ocean in the summertime. Jonathan smiled at the sensation. Even though he recognized he was out of his head, Jonathan still couldn't pull it together. He was so tired.

"Ooh, thank you," Jonathan cooed as the heat from the vent helped warm him a hair.

"Um, Jonathan. Your skin is glowing."

Jonathan didn't bother opening his eyes. "That's a sweet thing to say." It was too, since Jonathan had been nearly sucked dry by Dougal. He probably looked a pale mess with panda eyes. Lire should be complimenting him, though, since Jonathan had been saving his man. The funny thing was, he didn't feel like he was low on blood—just cold and exhausted. "I wish I had a blanket," Jonathan said more for himself as he waited for Lire to figure out how to heal Dougal. A soft weight landed on him, engulfing him in heat. Jonathan released a happy sigh. "Oh, that's nice. Thank you." He snuggled deeper beneath the soft cover.

"Um, darling," Niall said, obviously having returned from his hunt. "You might want to wake up and deal with the fact you're glowing like the sun and you've sprouted wings."

Okay. That was an odd thing to say. Jonathan peeked one eye open. A large feathery blanket covered him from shoulder to foot. The soft-looking cover moved. Jonathan felt it happen behind his shoulders. Panic shot through him. He sprang upward. His face hit the ceiling with enough force to knock him back to the bed with a bounce. Jonathan cupped his soon to be black eye and assessed his situation.

"I had better not have just flown," he said. His voice came out muffled around him nursing his injured face.

Three shocked stares faced him, including Dougal, who'd obviously awoken for the show. Niall cleared his throat. "You flew."

Goddamn it. "I flew," Jonathan agreed, incapable of softening his dry tone or denying what had just taken place. "Now I'm sitting on my wings," Jonathan added, trying not to flip out. "I shouldn't know that, but it hurts. Would someone like to explain why I have wings to sit on?"

"You're a Nephilim," Lire supplied unhelpfully.

Lire shouldn't have spoken. He really shouldn't have. Rage hit Jonathan. He dropped his hand and glared at Lire. "*You*. I don't know how or why, but this is all on *you*."

"Me?"

"You," Jonathan repeated. "I was in bed, wrapped in

my men's arms without any fucking wings before you showed up. Now I'm a goddamn bird."

"Nephilim," Lire repeated, as if reminding Jonathan of the truth.

Jonathan slashed his hand through the air. "What the fuck ever. I want these wings gone." In spite of his best efforts, Jonathan roared the final word, making everyone jump as his voice echoed off the walls, sounding unnatural. The wings shrank and disappeared. Jonathan watched it happen, still trying to fight back his panic. Once they were gone, he twisted, trying to see his back. There were black markings on his shoulders, but that was all he could see without a mirror. Niall circled the bed and inspected Jonathan's back.

"Whoa, baby. That's incredibly sexy."

Jonathan kept twisting at different angles. "What?"

"Come on," Niall said, helping him from the bed and heading for the dresser. There was a huge mirror above it. Jonathan turned and looked over his shoulder. He had wings tattooed on his back. They covered the entire surface, even disappearing beneath the back of his shorts. "We should go home. I'm verra interested in inspecting all of this," Niall said. Heat dripped from every word. Their gazes met and Jonathan didn't doubt his power to command everything in the universe. With a snap of his fingers, they were back home and in bed. The fake shorts Lire created were gone. Niall glanced around the room. "You did this?"

Jonathan didn't look away. He craved his mate. "Yes. I wanted to be home with you and knew I could have it, so I made it happen."

Niall shook his head. "I'll never stop being blown away by you."

Jonathan's mouth turned up in one corner. "The only thing stopping me from a total meltdown right now is this," Jonathan admitted, reaching out and stroking Niall's chest. Jonathan sent out a mental call for Cin, needing to complete their soul.

Cin, come home.

His sexy mate appeared like dust gathering in one spot until it formed the shape of Cin. He stared down at Jonathan and Niall from the edge of the bed. His gaze moved over Jonathan's face. Jonathan could feel the tickle of him probing his mind. Cin's eyes widened as Jonathan let him see as much as he liked. He climbed on the bed and inspected Jonathan's body. "Holy hell. That's hot," Cin said, tracing the lines of Jonathan's ink wings. The odd thing was, he felt it as if the man had touched the actual wings and not just a drawing.

"Fuck me," Jonathan moaned against his will. "Do that again."

At his demand, Cin traced the same line. A cry

escaped Jonathan. Cin's sexy blue eyes lit. "You have a new hot spot. I wonder what happens if I lick it."

Jonathan pushed at Niall's chest, forcing him onto his back. He straddled Niall's hips, even as he begged Cin not to stop. "There's only one way to find out." The final word left Jonathan's lips on a strangled cry as Cin's tongue stroked his spine. "Damn, I want you both inside me." These men—these sexy as sin otherworldly beasts—were his. Sometimes it struck Jonathan at the oddest times. Like now. He should be terrified and freaking the fuck out, but neither emotion took hold. Jonathan already knew—no matter what— he wasn't alone. As always, with every new power he randomly had thrust upon him, Jonathan turned to the pieces of his soul to remind him he was still just a man.

Cin stripped as Jonathan claimed Niall's mouth. Impatience roared through him as he shredded Niall's clothes, leaving the man nude. Cin's palm slid down Jonathan's spine. He lifted into the man's touch while never breaking Niall's kiss. Niall was dark. Inky blackness always brewed inside him just beneath the surface, but his kiss never showed it. His lips were soft and his tongue sweetly searching. Cin was the opposite. While Niall's kiss showed the man's gentle side—a side only Jonathan and Cin saw—Cin's lube-coated fingers stretched Jonathan's asshole, preparing him for the rough fucking he was about to receive.

Niall hissed as Cin took control and oiled up his

cock. Their mouths moved over every inch of one another's bodies they could reach as Cin helped guide Niall's dick inside Jonathan. Niall moaned. Jonathan gasped. He wanted everything they did to him. Jonathan couldn't pretend he wasn't kinky as fuck. Vampires' bodies were constantly repairing themselves, making moments such as these always feel like the first time. The idea of both his mates pushing their way inside him at the same time, finding his limits and pushing him over, had Jonathan's dick dripping pre-cum all over Niall's abs. They didn't need to touch his cock. His mind was fucked every bit as much as his ass and Jonathan was a mess.

He sank down on Niall's erection even as Cin fingered his hole, making room to guide his cock inside. Jonathan pushed back, needing the pain and the pleasure.

"Goddamn, baby," Cin hissed as he filled Jonathan past completion. "I don't know if I can move. Between this tight arse and Niall's sexy dick rubbing mine, I'm too close. Fook, you both slay me." Jonathan panted out each breath. Their cocks, Cin's words, and Niall's lips against his throat had Jonathan on the verge of flying apart. Then, Niall rotated his hips, pumping inside him. Jonathan saw stars. Cin cursed in three languages. "Oh, god. My babies," Cin hissed. He pivoted his hips, going deep and wiping Jonathan's mind clean. The way his men handled his body was the only thing Jonathan knew. "You make me want to bind you both and take my pleasure," Cin said, keeping up the torture. "The things I could do to you both, damn." His fangs sank into Jonathan's shoulder and all the images inside Cin's head filled Jonathan's mind. Cin's fantasies had Niall and Cin ass to ass, fucking a double-sided dildo while Jonathan held their dicks upright and sank down onto them over and over. The vision changed and Jonathan clung to the headboard while straddling Cin's head and balls deep down the man's throat while Niall fucked Cin's ass. They had forever—literally. There was nothing they weren't willing to try. In his human years, Jonathan had always been a bottom and nothing more. Eternity had expanded his willingness to try new things. Cin's fantasies had him wanting everything right now. Niall's fangs pierced his chest. The sudden pain combined with his mates holding him in place as they took their pleasure, making Jonathan's mind reel. Two dicks moved inside him, pulling him in every direction and hitting all the spots he loved. Cin's dirty thoughts kept overtaking him, moving from getting sucked off to him gagging on Cin's dick and hours of edging. Jonathan couldn't take any more. He fisted his cock and tugged. Release was right there just out of his reach. Still, Jonathan teased himself, toying with his crown and making his nerve endings sing before fucking his fist. In two short strokes, an explosion roared through him, tearing a shout from his throat. Everything went black as Niall moaned against his chest and Cin's cries vibrated against his neck. They collapsed into a heap.

3

*J*onathan loved playing with Cin's hair. As much as he enjoyed running his fingers through the dark locks, it was the small hairs on the back of his neck that always fascinated Jonathan. They were just long enough for him to curl around the tip of his finger. Every time he did it, chill bumps rose on Cin's skin. The third time it happened, Cin shivered and Niall's low chuckle caressed the side of Jonathan's neck.

"You're determined not to let the man sleep." The vibration of Niall's deep voice felt fucking amazing against Jonathan's skin.

As hard as he tried, Jonathan couldn't wipe away his smile. "I can't stop," he confessed on a whisper. Cin shifted closer, as if urging Jonathan on, so he did it again. Before Cin and Niall, he hadn't known a person could feel this much love. Sometimes, he thought it would burst from him in a huge wave of light, leveling everything in his path. He also had more to lose than anyone else alive. "I'm scared of all these changes," Jonathan whispered, keeping his voice low enough he wouldn't have his feelings hurt if they didn't hear. Of course, since they were vampires, there wasn't a chance of that happening.

Cin rolled, facing him. Damn, those iridescent blue eyes always punched him in the gut. "What are you afraid you'll become?"

Jonathan's shoulder lifted in a half shrug. "Something neither of you could love." His eyes burned at the confession. It was the first time he'd said the words aloud. "That's the only thing I couldn't live with."

Niall's hold tightened on Jonathan's waist. His hot breath caressed Jonathan's neck. "My fear is a little different," Niall said, his voice rumbling as if he was half asleep. "You gave away almost all your blood tonight and haven't needed us. What if you never need us again?"

Against his will, Jonathan snorted. He didn't want to make light of Niall's insecurities, but nothing could be further from the truth. "Nothing on Earth or in Heaven could make me not need either of you. You're everything to me."

Cin's mouth lifted in one corner. "Exactly. That's

why you shouldn't worry over these changes. There's nothing you could become that would change how we feel. This is love. We are permanent. You need to get some sleep."

While trying to smother his smile, Jonathan dutifully closed his eyes. A low knock sounded on the door. Niall growled as he rolled from the bed, heading for the door. "I swear if this is Faol asking to join us or some stupid bullshit, I'm locking him in a vampire trap for two weeks without food and water."

Jonathan swallowed back a chuckle. His clan gave zero fucks about walking around nude for the world to see. Jonathan hadn't lost his modesty yet. He pulled the covers over him before Niall threw the door open, bare-assed.

"Dougal," Niall said, sounding as shocked as Jonathan felt. "You're home."

Dougal wore only a ragged kilt, and he rubbed his arms like a crack addict. He looked like hell—dark circles marred his eyes and Jonathan swore he'd lost weight.

"Is it okay if I talk to Jonathan?"

Cin's thoughts hit Jonathan first. He was glad to see Dougal up and home, but pissed off everyone kept wanting so much from Jonathan. Niall's thoughts were almost an exact match. Jonathan's head just hurt. Now that he'd come down from the high of being serviced by his mates, Jonathan's night was catching up to him. He'd sprouted wings. That was huge. He'd also given Dougal almost all his blood but hadn't needed to replenish. That was kind of freaking him out too. Not to mention, he'd been glowing, which he hadn't even let breach his mind's shit-togetherness wall.

Still, Dougal looked like death. Jonathan climbed from the bed, taking the sheet with him as he went and wrapping it around his body like a toga. "Come on, babe. Let's find your bedroom, and we'll talk." Dougal stepped back as Jonathan headed for the hall. He tossed a look over his shoulder before leaving his men behind. "Love you guys. Get some sleep. I'll be back soon."

Without waiting for a response, Jonathan headed down the hall. He could feel Dougal on his heels. Something didn't feel right, but nothing had been as it should for as long as Jonathan could remember. "We put your stuff in this room at the end of the hall. I didn't know if you'd want it and didn't know how to ask." He opened the bedroom. "We kept it clean just in case." Dougal's silence made Jonathan want to fill the air with useless info.

"Are you taller than last time I saw you?" Dougal asked, finally breaking the silence.

A wave of exhaustion overcame Jonathan. "Fuck if I know." He pulled the covers back for Dougal because the man looked on the verge of death. "I'm damn tired of trying to figure out what all is happening with me. So, what's happening with you? Why are you back?"

Dougal climbed beneath the covers. "Lire said you told him to save me and he only knew one way. Then, he snapped his fingers, and I was back here."

A long, low sigh escaped Jonathan. He pinched the spot between his eyes where a new pain bloomed. "That stubborn... I can't even... that's not what I meant."

"I know." As Dougal made the claim, his teeth chattered. The sound pulled at Jonathan's heartstrings. If Cin or Niall sent him away, Jonathan might choose to curl in a ball and die. There'd be nothing left for him. Dougal and Lire weren't blood mates, but they were more than lovers. Jonathan could feel everyone and everything. What the pair had felt a lot like beauty hidden beneath mud.

"I'll fix this," Jonathan promised as he urged Dougal over and climbed in bed beside him. "Now, come here."

Dougal rolled into Jonathan's arms, letting Jonathan know he was right. This was why the man had come to him. Jonathan closed his eyes and concentrated on Dougal's pain. Dougal was too weak to keep him out. The man's brain was a crazy hot mess of sick need. Jonathan didn't know whether to laugh or cry because—if he really thought about it — he felt the same about Cin and Niall. The difference was, Jonathan's men weren't demons.

While keeping his eyes pressed closed, Jonathan worked at soothing away the jagged edges inside Dougal's mind. "Goddess Celeste doesn't make mistakes."

Dougal snorted. "You'd never heard of her before meeting us."

"She's my great-grandmother."

The way Dougal flew to his elbow, leaning over Jonathan, looking beyond shocked as he eyed Jonathan with disbelief, said so much—like Lire hadn't been sharing any secrets with Dougal. His features softened as if he found what he'd been searching for while staring at Jonathan. "I'm nay surprised, really. That detail actually explains a lot—like the wings and why you're the only one who makes the withdrawals bearable." Dougal settled back down, resting his head on Jonathan's chest.

Jonathan went back to staring at the inside of his eyelids. He focused on Dougal's barbed edges again. His arms lifted and his hands settled on Dougal. He soothed his palms down Dougal's back, as if ironing the wrinkles from Dougal's soul. Dougal shook. It hadn't been noticeable until Jonathan held him. The man's breathing was also ragged—like he'd run for miles.

"You're glowing again," Dougal said through

clenched teeth, as if trying to keep them from chattering again. Still, he somehow managed to sound tired.

Jonathan shushed him. "I can only deal with one thing at a time. If I don't see it, it isn't happening, and all is right in my world." Every word he spoke came out sounding overly Zen—like he could make the words true by using the power of his mind. He took a deep breath and focused harder on Dougal. While Jonathan searched for a way to fix things, Dougal's memories slipped over Jonathan. The farther back the memories went, the darker they became—like digging into the back of a closet where the light wasn't as strong. No matter how far back he went, one face always stood out. There was one person in Dougal's life who shone brighter than the rest. Their image clearer. "I can fix this," Jonathan whispered. "Just go to sleep, sweetie." Dougal's shaking stopped and his breathing evened out. Once he was certain Dougal was asleep, Jonathan slipped from the bed. He had a lot to do if he hoped to fix this mess.

HE WAS HOLLOW. For a long time, Dougal kept his eyes shut and his mind empty. He didn't know how long he'd slept. It didn't matter. He wasn't ready to climb from the bed. Everyone under this roof mattered to him. They'd pretend nothing happened, as if they'd seen him yesterday. He would pretend he wasn't dead inside. Life would go on. But he hurt. To his bones, Dougal ached and shook. The backs of his eyes felt like sandpaper and his nose stung. His throat was tight and his chest heavy. His limbs numb.

Dougal was old enough to know this would pass. He'd seen enough years to know the seasons. Damn, he was tired. He'd lived seven lifetimes and had forgotten more years than he remembered. Before now, he hadn't realized he was jaded. Turned out, he could still learn something new.

Calling on strength he didn't know he possessed, Dougal opened his eyes. His gaze landed on an expensive pair of boots attached to long legs. His gaze followed the hairy tree trunks to a chair beside the bed. Red hair and amethyst eyes waited there. With a white t-shirt stretched across his barrel chest and their clan's kilt covering his lower half, Faolan looked bored.

"You're awake," Faolan said, pointing out the obvious.

"Do you have your nasty boots on my bed?"

"No," Faolan said, blatantly lying. "They're Jonathan's," he added with a huge belly laugh that brought a smile to Dougal's face. It was short lived.

Dougal felt the burst of happiness slip from him, then die. "You don't have to watch over me. No one is coming for me."

Faolan crossed his arms over his massive chest and tilted the chair back on two legs. "We both know that's not what I'm worried about."

With a nod, Dougal closed his eyes. It was true. The real danger wasn't what someone else might to do to him. He tried clearing his mind. No peace would come. "Faol."

"Aye."

"Do you still hate me?"

For a moment, Dougal wondered if Faolan would answer his pointless question. When he finally spoke, Faolan's voice came out so low, he was near to whispering. "Aye. Every single day."

Dougal's eyes opened. Faolan's amethyst gaze was locked on him. Hot tears pressed at the backs of Dougal's eyes, but he refused to let them fall. He wanted to cry and cry until dehydration carried him into the next life. Surely Goddess Celeste knew he was no more than a plague and would eventually smite him. First, he'd endure a lifetime of torture. He deserved all of it. "You shouldn't care what happens to me."

"Hating you is all I have," Faolan said, making Dougal's chest ache even worse than before.

"Aye, I know. Would you hold me?"

Faolan dropped his feet to the floor before leaning forward and unlacing his boots. He didn't meet Dougal's gaze as he toed them off. Neither of them said a word as Faolan climbed onto the bed and gathered Dougal into his arms. Dougal shamelessly buried his nose against Faolan's chest and inhaled the man's familiar scent. Faolan's hatred was better than nothing. At least it was real, and Dougal could touch it. Dougal didn't have anything else either.

4

*G*uilt ate at Dougal when he spotted Jonathan slumped over in a chair at the kitchen table. His laptop along with several books spread across the table. The man's new wings folded around him like a warm blanket. They were black and long enough they draped to the floor.

Dougal quietly pulled out a chair and sat. He couldn't stop staring at the man who'd changed their clan. They'd survived centuries before their new prince joined them. It was almost funny how Dougal couldn't remember depending on anyone more. The moment Lire had dumped him back with his clan, Jonathan had been the first person he'd sought. Even though he'd been half out of his mind, he remembered clearly he wouldn't accept blood from anyone else, and Jonathan had saved his life. Pain sliced through

Dougal. Lire felt farther away by the second. It was as if he could physically feel Lire slipping away. He had to stop himself from waking Jonathan. It was black inside his head. No matter how hard he tried holding his shit together, his thoughts and emotions continued their downhill spiral.

Dougal tried concentrating on something else. He eyed the man who was mated to his prince. It had been close to five hundred years since angels had walked the earth. Jonathan's new wings were the same, but Lire had called him a Nephilim. That explained a lot. Most of his kind didn't come into their powers until later in life, if at all. Most grew stronger every day once the first powers showed themselves. Mentally, Jonathan seemed to be holding up well. Physically, Jonathan looked exhausted. He had dark circles under his eyes. Jonathan was truly a beautiful man inside and out. Dougal wasn't surprised he'd snagged two of his clansmen's hearts.

"There he is," Niall said, setting his hands on Dougal's shoulders and squeezing. Dougal immediately cleared his mind. As their prince, Niall could hear everyone's thoughts. No one could keep him out. Dougal didn't want anyone inside his head. "I wondered why he didn't come back to bed last night."

Jonathan shot up straight in his chair at Niall's words. His wings immediately disappeared as he blinked at the room as if trying to figure out where he was. The sheet he'd been wearing the night before pooled in Jonathan's lap, barely hiding anything. Against his will, Dougal's gaze swept Jonathan's body. Jonathan wasn't his type, but he was beautiful, especially lightly glowing like a god as he was now.

Jonathan focused on Dougal while still looking slightly confused. "Hi."

Everything fell away. A smile tugged at the corners of Dougal's mouth. "Hi."

Jonathan's green gaze moved to Niall. His features softened. "Sorry. I must've fallen asleep."

A loud weary-sounding sigh filled the kitchen. With one sound, Niall managed to sound like the most put-upon husband on the planet. "No more work for you," Niall said, circling the table and sweeping Jonathan into his arms. "You're going to bed and I don't care if the house is under attack. You're not leaving until you've had a full eight hours of sleep."

After wrapping his arms around Niall's neck, Jonathan buried his face against it. The move did nothing to muffle his voice. "Okay, baby, but Dougal has to go back to bed too."

Dougal bit back a groan as Niall paused beside his chair. Niall's golden gaze locked on Dougal. "You heard the man. Back to bed. Everyone in this house is on their last leg. I'm declaring this a lazy day. Everyone get in the bed."

Faolan passed through the kitchen, obviously

catching the last of Niall's order. His usual faked bright smile made an appearance. He clapped and rubbed his hands together. "Sweet. I've been waiting for the annual orgy."

Niall scoffed. Jonathan's low chuckle filled the room. It was all the encouragement Faolan needed. "I'll grab the lard and eggplants."

"Oh, god," Jonathan choked out, burying his face tighter against Niall's throat. "I don't even want to know."

The chuckle escaping Dougal surprised even him. "He's just fucking with you, sweets."

"Or am I?" Faolan asked, waggling his eyebrows. Since Niall had his back to Faolan, heading for the door, obviously done with his antics, a lump formed in Dougal's throat. It had been a damn long time since Faol tried making him laugh.

Faolan moved to the table and claimed the chair Jonathan vacated. "Let's see what our genius has been researching." Dougal chewed on his nails as Faolan flipped through the books. "Demonology. Four demon-themed romance books. Two on demon sickness. These are all fiction. He needs to find a local Catholic Church if he wants to research demons."

Dougal pressed his palm on the table, trying to focus on Faolan's words and hang on to his shit. Jonathan was trying to fix him. Dougal wasn't as sure there was a cure. A slash of red caught his eye and

Dougal dropped his gaze to the table. His fingernails were gone. The tip of his fingers bled freely. He stared at his hand—detached. The silence of the room penetrated his fogged mind. Dougal glanced up to find Faolan staring at his hands. Their gazes met.

Anger flashed in Faolan's eyes. "You're always a slave to some monster's dick."

There it was—Faolan's hatred, stabbing him through the heart at the perfect moment. The air rushed from Dougal's lungs as Faolan's mental blow hit its mark. Hot tears pressed at his eyes. Dougal flew to his feet. His chair crashed to the floor.

As Dougal hovered over him, Faolan deflated before his eyes. "I shouldn't have said that."

Dougal's chest burned with too many painful emotions for him to choose one. "Aye, you should've. You're right. All I'll ever be is a slave." If Faolan had a retort, Dougal would never know. He dissipated and reappeared inside his bedroom. His gaze flew around the room, searching for something to destroy. Nothing looked satisfying enough. The only thing in the room that would bring him relief would be demolishing himself. Dougal unwound his kilt and dropped it to the floor before moving to stand in front of the mirror hanging on the back of his bedroom door.

Today, he looked different—diminished. Without Lire feeding his addiction, Dougal's rough treatment showed. Vampires rarely scarred. They healed too fast.

Unfortunately, a demon's bite left a mark. Their venomous serrated teeth tore at the skin and poisoned the blood, leaving behind scarred skin. Those light white marks marred his neck. Proving how sick and twisted Dougal had become as Lire's captive, Dougal's dick stirred at the sight of them. He could still feel Lire's teeth tearing into his neck as his cock stretched his ass. There was so much pleasure in the pain.

A thin layer of sweat broke out across his body. Dougal stared at his reflection as he ran his hand down his stomach. His eyes followed his hand's progress as it headed for the erection tapping at his navel. It wouldn't be the same. Lire wasn't there, coating the air with his magic. Dougal's mind wouldn't fog with Lire's whispered spells and dirty talk. He smoothed his palm down his cock. His nerve endings sang. It mattered Lire was gone, and he was alone, but then again, it didn't. Lire had done his job as a lilin demon. He'd addicted Dougal to sex, corrupting his mind from all purpose and ruining his body for all others. The addiction to sex would be lifelong and that was a damn severe punishment for a vampire. He'd agreed—a life for a life. At the time, he hadn't known what he'd promised. All Dougal wanted was to save Jonathan. Demons were tricky. Wording was everything. Lire hadn't said a death for a death or a soul for a soul. No, he'd said a life for a life. Jonathan had lived. So too would Dougal —forever cursed to the madness.

Pre-cum rolled down Dougal's dick. He rolled his hips into his touch as he two-handed himself. Dougal jacked his dick and squeezed his balls. He needed a second of peace. The only place he'd find it was in the seconds of release when he died a little.

Loosening his knees, Dougal fucked his fist. He was shameless as he watched his cock slide up and down in his tight hold in the mirror. His teeth sank into his bottom lip, stifling his cries. He could do this forever—stay on the edge where pain didn't exist. There were toys packed away somewhere. He could break them out, lock himself away, and fuck himself until he passed out from exhaustion. When the torturous addiction woke him, he could start all over again. He didn't need Lire. He didn't need... his heart cried out in denial before another name could cross his mind, but it left his lips as the growing pressure exploded into waves of ecstasy, coating the mirror in cum. Dougal gasped through each wave, squeezing out each drop until his shoulders heaved from the effort.

For a moment, he stared at his jizz-covered reflection. A familiar thought sneaked in. He was home. This was the real him. The way men saw him—broken and with cum coating his face. As Faolan had said—always someone's cock slave. A burst of rage exploded from him. Dougal's fist connected with the mirror and kept flying out until his knuckles ripped to shreds and the mirror turned to dust. His entire body shook, but his mind cleared. Dougal was done. He'd given almost seven hundred years of service, and too many pieces of himself to count. It was over.

ALL JONATHAN COULD FIND to wear was a pair of workout shorts. He didn't bother with a shirt. The second he'd put one on, his wings had popped out, shredding parts of the material while getting trapped by the remnants. If he'd thought his body had behaved like a hormonal teenager's after turning vampire, that was nothing compared to this. He intermittently got taller, and then shorter. When he'd walked past the bathroom mirror and caught sight of his reflection, his eyes had been two different colors— one green and one gold. Not just any gold either. His eye had looked like a melted pot of leprechaun gold. It was eerie as hell. One day soon, he'd never be allowed in public again, except at conventions and on Halloween.

He'd taken to pacing the den. Cin and Niall watched him, walking a hole into the carpet, while wearing matching stoic expressions. Jonathan wasn't fooled. He knew he looked like something out of a cartoon—one wing hanging out and fangs refusing to retract.

"I'd say you look more like a drunken angel coming

home from one hell of a party," Niall said, obviously reading his thoughts.

Jonathan shot him a dirty look. "Now's probably not a good time to be in my head."

"Aye, I skimmed that fuck you that you sent my way right then, but you know I can't help it if you're not blocking me."

"I don't have the energy to block you." Even Jonathan heard the exhaustion in his tone. His cellphone rang once, then fell silent. Jonathan crossed the room to where he'd left it on the table. Any distraction at all was welcome. A New York area code from an unknown number showed on the face. He swiped it away. "Wrong number, I guess."

Cin patted the empty spot on the couch. "Come sit with us. Faolan is making us coffee. There's nothing you can do but wait out all the craziness your body is putting you through. Stressing isn't helping anything."

Faolan appeared in the doorway, carrying their drinks, before Jonathan could respond. He handed Niall and Cin coffee mugs before passing him a juice box. "And juice for the young one in the bunch."

"Ha. Ha," Jonathan said, stabbing the straw into the box. "Shows what you know. I like juice boxes." Jonathan moved to the window and looked out, because literally no one looked like an adult, taking the high road, while drinking from a tiny straw. His vision automatically switched to night mode, lighting the back yard outside the window like it was noon.

"It's a good thing you like sucking on small things since you chose Cin and Niall over me."

A movement beneath the window caught Jonathan's eye. He leaned closer to the pane. "It's a good thing you..." Dougal carried a pile of wood to an already blazing inferno of debris. "What the... Um, why is Dougal building a bonfire out back?"

"What?" Faolan snapped, sounding panicked.

"In the back yard," Jonathan repeated, motioning toward the window. "He has a fire—" A loud crash sounded behind him. Jonathan spun. Three coffee cups were smashed upon the floor and the men were gone. Spinning, Jonathan checked the backyard. Niall, Cin, and Faolan appeared on the lawn, running full speed in Dougal's direction. After tossing his juice box aside, Jonathan ran for the back door, nearly ripping it off its hinges. He got there just in time to see Faolan snag Dougal from behind, lifting him off his feet at the edge of the fire.

Faolan kept Dougal in an iron grip with the man's back against his chest while Dougal fought against his hold. Jonathan watched the entire scene with two parts confusion and one part horror.

"You can't do this to me," Faolan yelled at the top of his lungs as if trying to break through Dougal's madness. "I lied, okay. I lied. All those times I said I hate you, it wasn't true. I hate me. Not you. I hate me."

Dougal went limp in Faolan's hold. "It's a warrior's death. There's no shame in that," Dougal whispered. Jonathan heard the words as if he'd screamed them. Everything clicked inside Jonathan's head. His shock slowed his brain. Dougal had intended to kill himself. While they'd all stood inside the den, drinking coffee and joking, Dougal had intended to burn himself alive. Jonathan bent at the waist, set his hands on his knees, and sucked air. It was a shot to the chest. He hadn't helped. All the digging into Dougal's brain the night before, hoping to bring the man relief, had done nothing. Lire was right. Dougal couldn't be fixed. Lire couldn't help him and Jonathan couldn't fix anyone. He was useless. Faolan kept speaking in low tones, trying to talk Dougal off the ledge. "No, baby. There's no shame in that, but I'm not ready for you to go. You can't leave me behind. We're supposed to go together. Remember? We swore we'd go together."

"I'm tired, Faol. No one sees me. I can't be the slave anymore."

"Shhh," Faolan soothed. "I never should've said that. You've always been our guardian, sacrificing yourself for us. Let us take care of you for once. You've always taken the punishment so the rest of us would be spared. Let us fix you. Don't leave me."

Jonathan, it has to be you. Dougal won't let anyone else

help him. Niall sounded so calm, as if he knew for a fact Jonathan could help Dougal. Jonathan straightened. His mind cleared. Niall believed. It didn't matter if Jonathan did. With every step in Dougal's direction, Jonathan grew larger. His wings unfurled, dragging the ground behind him. By the time he faced Dougal, he was staring down at the man. As usual, Jonathan pretended it wasn't happening. He was still himself, only different.

Dougal met his gaze. There was so much pain and hopelessness in the man's eyes, it broke through something inside Jonathan. The puzzle inside Jonathan's head snapped together. He saw everything for what it was. "You need to come with me, Dougal."

As if further proving how far gone Dougal was, he didn't question Jonathan. Faolan released the man, and he walked into Jonathan's outstretched arms. Jonathan's wings engulfed the broken vampire. The air sizzled and popped around them. He closed his eyes and took Dougal away. The moment the air turned cool and their feet touched solid ground, Jonathan released Dougal.

"Why did you bring me here?"

The dead note to Dougal's voice had Jonathan questioning his reasoning. He couldn't back down now. "Lire isn't here," Jonathan promised. "Now is your chance. Do what you want. Smash his shit. Get angry. Want to burn his house to the ground? I'll help. Just get mad at the right person and stop torturing yourself." With every word Jonathan spoke, he felt like the world's biggest asshole. That was what Dougal needed right now.

Dougal turned in a circle. Everything was the same in the bedroom as it had been the last time Jonathan had been there, making him wonder if Lire had returned at all since he'd dumped Dougal back with the clan.

Dougal's silence was too much. Jonathan didn't have the same self-control. "I'll find some scissors if you want to shred his clothes."

Rather than laughing or exploding as Jonathan hoped, Dougal set his knee on the mattress and climbed onto the bed. On his stomach, he hugged a pillow to his chest and inhaled. Jonathan's eyes burned. Dougal's pain was real and choking. Jonathan climbed in next to him, hugged the man's waist, and hung on.

"He's not real," Dougal said, finally breaking the silence and saying what Jonathan already knew. "Not really."

"I know."

"What did he look like to you?"

Damn, Jonathan hated this. "Shaggy brown hair, ever-changing eyes, and tattooed chest."

Dougal swallowed so hard Jonathan heard it. "He had long dark curly hair and copper eyes. They were unnatural and beautiful. Sleeve tattoos. Lip, nipples, and crown piercings. That was the real him, but I was the only one who saw him."

Jonathan nodded—unsurprised. "He told me to touch his hand while we had him trapped, and he'd show me everything. I did."

Dougal glanced over his shoulder. His expression called Jonathan a fool before his lips had time. "Idiot. He could've ripped you to pieces."

"I know," Jonathan said. He smiled, hoping he looked contrite. Honestly, he regretted nothing. "He didn't show me anything. Instead, he gave me a rose that transformed into a slip of paper. All it said was 'Port of Southern Louisiana.' At the time, I thought that was everything. It wasn't until after you were gone I realized the truth. He showed me nothing and gave me nothing. That was everything. Lire was showing me the truth. He is nothing."

Dougal settled back down. He nodded. "I noticed on the second day of torturing him. His reactions didn't match the situations. Sometimes, he would heal immediately. The next, it would take him a while. Sometimes, he would scream in pain. Other times, he'd laugh. He pretended ignorance about things any demon would know, even a spawn, which is exactly why we thought he was a younger and more human than demon."

"When, in truth, he's the seventh son of the seventh

prince of hell," Jonathan finished for him. "A pure demon with no corporeal body."

"Aye," Dougal said, sounding as if he'd turned inside himself. "He's no more than smoke, taking on whatever form we want to see. That's probably why— to you—his eyes were ever changing. You didn't know what you wanted to see when you looked at him." Dougal fell silent for so long, Jonathan didn't think he'd say anything more. Finally, he sucked in a deep breath. It sounded loud in the otherwise silent room. "Most of the time, when we were together, he looked like Faol."

Jonathan had never been more thankful in his life for someone not looking at him. He knew his shock showed. Rather than screeching about how he must know, Jonathan massaged Dougal's shoulders and searched his mind for a response. He'd known, after picking through the man's memories, Faolan's face stood out above all others. Jonathan had also seen Faolan's reaction when he thought Lire had killed Dougal. He needed more details. This wasn't something he could fix. Lire had been right about that. Dougal's soul was broken. Jonathan couldn't mend that. But he could be here and learn as many details as possible. Information is power. Jonathan intended to use it as such.

EVEN THOUGH DOUGAL could feel the shock rolling off Jonathan in waves, he didn't ask right away. Dougal had no idea why he'd confessed to such a thing. He was heartbroken and his soul ached. Those things had been true for centuries. This new thing—the damage he'd suffered from Lire—it broke something different inside him. It was like a dam bursting. Until now, he hadn't realized he'd possessed a single thing left to destroy. Lire had known and smashed him to bits with it.

Dougal wanted to roll and confess his weakness. He needed to look someone in the eye and say the words, making some part of Lire real. He'd loved him. It was stupid. In truth, his feelings were probably some form of fucked up Stockholm syndrome, even though he'd never been a prisoner of anything other than his word. No one would ever know what happened in this bed. By becoming Faolan, Lire had soothed his soul— his conscience. It wasn't Lire's fault he was addictive. No one could help how they were born. Lire was the son of Lust—literally. It was an inescapable fate. A curse. The true test of any man or beast was the choices he made. Lire had chosen to serve Goddess Celeste, but no matter how much good he did, Lire would always be nothing at all. Just a bodiless soul that tormented men. Fate had been so damn cruel to them both. Now the peaceful half of being with Lire was gone. All Dougal had left was the itch he couldn't scratch. Mental pain was a hell of thing. It was so real Dougal could damn near touch it, but he could never wipe it away. Since the madness was in his head, it seemed as if he could tell it to stop. He should get to choose what his brain thought and felt. Instead, he didn't belong to himself at all. Dougal was a slave in more ways than one.

When Jonathan's question finally came, it was almost a relief. "Tell me about Faolan."

Dougal soaked up Jonathan's touch. With his eyes closed and Jonathan rubbing his shoulders, Dougal thought over the question. "I'm not sure where to start with that one."

Jonathan's fingers dug into his shoulders. "Anywhere you want. Just say the first thing that pops in your head. I've found when writing a news story, that's where everything truly begins—with that first random detail."

Dougal took a deep breath, cleared his head, and tried not to think about it. An image of Faolan appeared in Dougal's mind. They'd been much younger and living in the stronghold. His smile was untainted. Dougal pressed his hand to his stomach to quell the butterflies. A smile tugged at his lips. He could remember every ridiculous skit the man did every night, entertaining the clan like a stand-up comedian. "He was once the greatest love of my life." Tears pricked at his eyes as he made the confession. He could still feel Jonathan's surprise. Dougal didn't let it slow him. "I don't know how much Niall has told you about our clan or our race, but being gay isn't acceptable. Not for blood mates anyhow." A derisive snort escaped Dougal. "Now that didn't stop Niall's father, Adair, from using his position as king to demand sexual favors from whoever he chose. I was his favorite." A chill raced down Dougal's spine. He shivered. The pressure on his shoulders increased as if Jonathan was trying to massage the memory away. In truth, it helped. He kept talking. "He would say my name." Dougal swallowed the bile rising in his throat at the memory. "I can't even describe it. Adair would caress my jaw and say my name. I knew immediately I'd be on my knees for the rest of the night."

"Was there any hope of saying no? Didn't he have a mate?"

Dougal shook his head. "Our world is different. There's no such thing as being born a bastard. Kings have children with the strongest women, hoping to create strong future kings. The rest of the time, they do as they please." Dougal had a thought and shrugged. "I suppose not all kings are that way, but I've only ever known the one. As one of the king's warriors, I was no more than a slave. I belonged to him in any way he chose to use me." Dougal swallowed as he tried not to consider all the possibilities. Still, he found himself confessing them to Jonathan. "If he was to show up tomorrow and demand I return, I'd have no choice but to go back to that horrible life. Except, this time, there'd be no Faolan to ease the pain. I'd watch him and dream," Dougal admitted, smiling in spite of the horrible topic. "One night, Adair had that look in his eyes, so I ducked into an empty alcove and hid. I knew it was only a temporary reprieve, but I couldn't stop myself. Adair is evil. He liked to make me hurt, and I was tired." A tear slipped from the corner of his eye as he made the confession. It landed on the arm beneath his head before dropping onto the bed. He'd never told anyone that before. Even though he was certain people had guessed what went on in Adair's bedroom, Dougal had never said the words. Adair was his king. It should've been an honor, but Dougal wanted to choose. He swiped his face on his arm. "I stood in the dark, trying to be me for half a second." Dougal snorted. "I guess that sounds ridiculous, but when you belong to someone else, you're never you. You're whatever they say you are." An unexpected smile touched Dougal's lips. "Faolan appeared in the doorway." Dougal could still remember the way his heart had skipped a beat.

Are you waiting for me?

Dougal's stomach muscles clenched at the memory. He hadn't been that time, but every other time after that, he'd been Faolan's man. The small amount of warmth he'd found at the memory slipped away. "If you think no one can hide anything from Niall, he doesn't hold a candle to his father. He could've chosen to kill me or Faolan, but he's too cruel for that. Instead, he made an arrangement with Faolan's sister. She would get me as her husband, a much better match than she could've hoped since I was a royal guard and she was a commoner. In exchange, she would look the other way when it was only his bed I warmed." It had been one hell of a calculated move. "He'd known, as his sister's husband, Faolan would never touch me again."

"Except Faolan did," Jonathan said, obviously taking a stab in the dark.

"Yes. Rose, Faolan's sister, caught us. She chose to walk into the fire and move on to the next life rather than face the humiliation. Faolan has never forgiven me. Nor should he. We've guarded our prince under the same roof for hundreds of years, but he doesn't stay in the same room with me for longer than five minutes at a time. He doesn't look at me or joke with me. For hundreds of years, I've been dead to him." Another tear joined the first on the bed. "When I was young, I would see old warriors willingly walk into the fire and it never failed to shock me. I couldn't imagine wanting to leave this life badly enough to endure that pain. Now I get it. Physical pain is nothing. It's the mind that controls your torture." Dougal closed his eyes and absorbed Jonathan's warmth. He didn't want the man to stop trying to comfort him, but they couldn't do this forever. "I'm fucked up, Jonathan. It's not your fault I can't be fixed. You're an amazing person. If I had to do it all over again, I'd still go with Lire. You will be an amazing king. I would've proudly served you."

"I won't be king, but thank you, and stop talking like you're leaving me."

Dougal swallowed, barely holding it together. "You will. Lire said that's why you're so important. I assumed you knew."

Jonathan's hands froze where they rubbed Dougal's back. "That's the first I've heard of it." He heard Jonathan take a deep breath behind him—like he was practicing meditation. "I can only deal with one issue at a time," Jonathan said, sounding like it was meant more for himself and he was giving himself permission to not be perfect. In spite of everything, Dougal smiled. Jonathan was amazing and funnier than he realized. Jonathan blew out a sigh. "Okay," he said. "Let's get back on track."

Dougal rolled. Jonathan needed someone too, but he spread himself thin for everyone else. "Are you scared?"

The man's usually green eyes glowed gold. His mouth lifted in one corner. "I'm fucking terrified. One day, I might not be me anymore. Niall and Cin don't think they can stop loving me, but..." Jonathan paused and shrugged. "Who knows?"

Dougal eyed the man's features. Right now, in all his Nephilim glory, Jonathan barely resembled the human Cin had introduced to them years ago. Dougal couldn't solve his own problems, but he understood loving someone, and it wasn't so easily broken. "If Niall or Cin woke up tomorrow with wings, two feet taller, and capable of controlling everything with their minds, would you feel differently about them?"

Jonathan's features remained blank. "Can I control everything with my mind?"

"What do you think?"

"I think Lire confessed more to you than you've let on," Jonathan said. "But I understand what you're getting at," he added. "I wouldn't feel differently about them. My love runs deeper than appearances and abilities. But, if what you say is true and I control everything, everyone will come for me. Not just Mammon, but everyone. That's a whole other reason for me to worry. Niall and Cin are already so worried about protecting me that they haven't been dealing with anything else."

Dougal nodded. It felt good to concentrate on someone else. His heartache eased with his focus on Jonathan. "You need a personal guard staying with you, so Niall and Cin can focus on figuring out Mammon's game."

Jonathan smiled. His eyes changed back to green. A lump formed in Dougal's throat. Jonathan felt like his friend. In truth, no one had felt like his friend in a long time. It wasn't anyone's fault but his. Still, he soaked up the moment. "Are you volunteering for the position?"

A sense of purpose rose in Dougal's chest. He'd been out of commission, playing the sex slave for too long. The clan had continued without him. He didn't have a place any longer. Jonathan offered him one now. Dougal hadn't lied earlier. He would be proud to have Jonathan as his king. The man was kind and would bring peace. "If you want my life, it's yours—such as it is."

"If you're giving me your life, you have to actually live."

Dougal smiled. It disappeared as quickly as it appeared. "I'm not one hundred percent. In truth, I'm not even fifty percent. It's pretty much fucked up monkeys clanging on drums in my brain right now while spiders crawl on my skin."

"Just give me time," Jonathan said, his heart in his eyes. "Promise to stay with me, and I'll find a way to make you better. I'd take ten percent of you over all the warriors in King Adair's clan."

"Okay." Even as Dougal agreed, he prayed he could keep his word. He felt halfway human right now, but he knew it wouldn't last.

5

They'd stayed a few hours longer after Dougal agreed to be his personal guard. Dougal needed that time to soothe his need for Lire. The addiction would be the worst part, but Jonathan hadn't lied. He'd take a broken Dougal over any other warrior guarding him on the planet. As they came through the back door, the house was unnaturally silent. He imagined the nonstop bullshit they'd endured over the last year had everyone exhausted.

"Do you want to zap into your bedroom and face everyone later?"

Dougal's jaw flexed, making him look hard. "No. I won't play the coward. Plus, you're my ward now. I'm supposed to be guarding you."

A chuckle escaped Jonathan. "I get the feeling I

should set some ground rules now before you try following me to the bathroom."

Dougal's laughter caught Jonathan off guard. His gaze slid the man's way as he stepped into the den, following his inner radar to get to his mates. Dougal focused on something over Jonathan's shoulder. His smile slipped away before he hit his knees. Jonathan's surprise made him slow to respond. For a moment, all he could do was stare at Dougal on his knees with his head bowed. He cast a desperate look around, searching for answers. Niall, Cin, and Faolan were on their knees, heads bowed and surrounded by armed men—one of which looked exactly like a more rugged version of Niall. He was a barrel-chested man with a slim waist and legs like tree trunks. Realization hit. This was Niall's father—the king. Rage followed. This was the man who'd imprisoned his clan and killed Niall's first mate. His crimes against Dougal were unforgivable. King or not, Dougal should've been given a choice.

Adair eyed Jonathan with open contempt. "You should be on your knees, or has no one told you about your king?"

A derisive snort sounded from Jonathan without a single thought. "You're no king of mine."

Three of Adair's men pulled swords from their backs. Jonathan experienced the oddest desire to laugh. Swords seemed so out of place. Adair motioned for his men to still. "You were an American when you were human. Now, you belong to me," Adair said, moving in Jonathan's direction. "The moment you became my son's mate, you fell under my rule." He didn't stop moving until he was toe to toe with Jonathan, forcing Jonathan to tilt his chin up to hold the man's stare.

A growl ripped through Jonathan's mind. It was Niall. Adair's gaze slid to Dougal at Jonathan's feet. The man's expression transformed into something Jonathan prayed he'd never see again. It sent chills down Jonathan's spine.

"Dougal."

Jonathan's stomach churned.

Adair's hand moved toward Dougal's jaw.

Jonathan snapped. His wings unfurled and Jonathan found himself staring at the top of Adair's head. His arm shot out, and he grabbed Adair's wrist before the man could touch Dougal. "You don't touch him. Not ever." Even Jonathan heard the demonic note to his voice as he felt the bones pop and crumble underneath his grip.

Despite the damage and the fact that Jonathan had gone full Nephilim on him, Adair didn't as much as flinch. "The sentence for defying your king is death." He struck out, punching Jonathan in the chest with his free arm. In a true testament to his rage, Jonathan didn't feel a thing. The blow was no more than a feather brushing over his skin.

"You'll never see me on my knees," Jonathan taunted.

Adair's men sprang forward. Cin and Niall flew to their feet, snarling with rage. Energy pulsed through the room, rocking Jonathan on his feet. To his surprise, everyone fell to their knees again, including Adair. Jonathan released him as he caught sight of the woman standing in the center of the room. Lire stood at her back. Dougal pulled at the hem of Jonathan's shorts, as if trying to pull Jonathan to the floor. Jonathan couldn't take his eyes off the woman who held his stare.

Jonathan stepped around Adair, moving toward her as if she reeled him closer with an invisible line. "I know your face," Jonathan said, incapable of speaking above a whisper. His throat was tight. Jonathan didn't love many people. He loved this woman.

A sweet smile touched her lips. Her green eyes, so much like his own, glowed with pride. She met him halfway. "Hi, Jonathan."

Jonathan couldn't help himself. He cupped her face. "I know you," he repeated—like he couldn't stop. He pulled her into a hug. Jonathan didn't need a response. He only needed to hug her. She hugged him back. Jonathan knew she would. Pulling away, his gaze moved over her face. He couldn't stop staring at her.

With a small laugh, she glanced down at Niall. While still clinging to Jonathan, she reached down and urged Niall to his feet. "Did you see that?" she asked, patting Niall's chest, "For the record, that was the perfect greeting for meeting someone who's loved you since before you were born. It's time," she said, holding Niall's gaze. Neither of them would meet Jonathan's stare. Jonathan cast a glance around, searching for answers. Everyone had their heads bowed or were looking elsewhere. Lire's focus was locked on Dougal. He stepped around Celeste and headed Dougal's way.

Lire reached down and held his hand out for Dougal. "It's okay, sexy. In Celeste's presence, there's no harm in touching me." Dougal's chin lifted. Their gazes met. Jonathan couldn't look away. The way they stared at each other tightened Jonathan's throat. Their palms met and Lire helped Dougal to his feet. "You don't bow here."

Jonathan was hit by a wave of anger coming from Adair. He was the king here. Yet he'd been left on his knees. Still, Jonathan couldn't stop clinging to Celeste. The last of his family had passed on years ago. Now she was here. It didn't matter he couldn't remember ever meeting her before now. He remembered her presence. She felt like his blood.

"What brings you here?" Jonathan asked before adding, "I'm sorry. I don't know what to call you."

Her smile was kind and Jonathan couldn't look away. "What do you feel in your heart?"

Jonathan pressed his lips together, trying to hide his smile. His thoughts bordered on ridiculous, but he couldn't stop the words from escaping. "Grandma Celeste."

A loud but beautiful laugh escaped her. He'd known it didn't make sense, because she looked even younger than him, but she'd asked. Jonathan had answered truthfully. "I love it," she said, surprising Jonathan with the honesty in her voice. "In fact, I've waited a very long time to hear you call me that." Her eyes filled with tears. She blinked them away. Jonathan couldn't stop taking in every detail. "My time here is always limited, but I've stayed away too long." After squeezing Jonathan's hand, she moved away to hover over Adair. "Back when I appointed the first kings to their posts, I thought it was such a grand idea. A system of checks and balances, needing little input from me. Vampires keeping watch over werewolves. Werewolves watching demons. Demons keeping shapeshifters in check. Everyone looking at everyone else and keeping each other from getting out of control. Ensuring humans were none the wiser. With a few exceptions," she said, flashing Jonathan a smile.

Her smile slipped away. She shook her head, making her dark curls bounce. "Kings were never meant to oppress or treat the world as their private playground. They were meant to help guide their people and bring together the perfect clan. Like this one," she said, waving toward where Jonathan, Niall, Cin, Faolan, and Dougal stood with Lire. "Strong, cunning, loving, and self-sacrificing while still finding the humor in life. You're the perfect example of what I hoped to achieve." She dropped her chin and stared down at Adair. "Somehow, I got this," she said, nodding toward Adair. "I've been watching you, Adair. Would you like to know what I've seen?"

Adair didn't respond.

Celeste didn't seem to need a reply. "I guess you know what I've seen," she said, sounding absent. "It's gone on long enough. I should've intervened long ago." She turned her head and focused on Dougal. A tear slid down her cheek. "The only excuse I have is that time moves differently in the heavens. Sometimes it's as if only a day has passed. In truth, it's been a century. I'm here now," she said, her voice growing stronger. Jonathan was afraid to blink. He could feel her power filling the room. The hairs on his arms stood. He recognized he was playing witness to a change in history. Jonathan just wasn't sure what would happen next.

Celeste caressed Adair's jaw, urging his chin up to meet her stare. Once she had his attention, the air shifted, turning ominous. Jonathan suppressed a shudder. Something bad was coming. "You struck my grandson. What do you have to say for yourself?"

"There are no words," Adair said, sounding contrite. "I didn't know."

Celeste paced the floor in front of him. "Yet you knew he was your son's mate. Still, you didn't hesitate striking him. Even if Jonathan wasn't my blood, that was beyond disrespectful. This is their home. Cin, Dougal, and Faolan are their men now. You have no rights here. This soil isn't yours. This isn't leadership. It's tyranny. Not to mention, Jonathan *is* my blood. I cannot overlook your slight. Tell me what I'm supposed to do with you now."

"I don't know, your Grace."

"What would you do if a mangy dog bit your child?"

Adair's predicament became clearer by the second. His punishment inescapable. The way his men tried inching away and making themselves smaller was a true testament of how they didn't wish to share in their king's fate. "I would put it down, my Grace. However," he said, impressing Jonathan with his gall. "We're not talking about a mangy dog. I'm one of your appointed kings. Surely that affords me some leniency."

"Jonathan is also a chosen king."

"What?" Adair asked.

Jonathan echoed him. "What?"

Celeste nodded as if the gesture was meant more

for herself. "The Americas have been left unattended too long. With Jonathan coming into his full powers, there's no one better to handle its rule. He's strong, smart, loving, and of my blood. There's no one else, period. Not that it'll matter to you," Celeste said, her pacing coming to an end as she towered over Adair. "Your time has come to an end. I'd like to say you've served me well, but alas..." She stepped back and waved an absent hand at Adair. He crumpled to the floor. Dead.

Jonathan blinked at the sight. His tongue froze to the roof of his mouth. She'd declared him king. Even with Dougal's warning, he hadn't been prepared. He wanted to scream at the top of his lungs that he had no clue what he was doing. Jonathan had no business being king. What the hell did vampire kings even do? When he'd found himself mated to a prince, he'd damn near hyperventilated, and then he'd had no chance of ascending. Now, he was a fucking king. It was surreal—like he was watching everything happen to someone else through distorted glass.

Celeste touched his cheek. All his doubts slipped away, settling into an inner peace he'd never experienced. "You'll never be alone," she promised with a sweet smile. "This place needs your loving hand, but not much else. The community here has formed a democracy in the absence of leadership. Lend them your strength. Everything else will fall into place. Trust your blood mates and clan. Most of all, know that I love you, and I'm always listening." She took a step back and glanced around. After focusing on the nearest member of Adair's clan, she motioned toward the dead king's body. "Take your king home but remember what you've learned here. I'm watching."

With a nod, the man nearest to Adair grabbed his body and disappeared. In the blink of an eye, the room was empty of unwanted guests. Niall's fingers linked with his. Cin took his other hand. They were a team. Celeste was right. He'd never be alone. Jonathan glanced around at their unlikely family. He loved everyone in this room. More likely than not, he'd fail at this king business, but he already knew they wouldn't think less of him when he did.

Celeste eyed them and smiled. "I couldn't have chosen three better men to rule together." She stopped just short of happy clapping, but Jonathan thought it was understood. Celeste cast Lire a glance. "Kiss your man goodbye. It'll likely be a long time before you can do so with your own lips and not make him crazy."

Jonathan had no idea what that was supposed to mean, but Lire jumped at the chance to touch his lips to Dougal's. Faolan looked away as if he couldn't watch. Jonathan puffed out his cheeks and blew out a sigh. Soon Celeste would leave, and he still didn't know how to fix the mess that they had become. All he could do was hope. In truth, hope was his only solid plan. They were all fucked.

DOUGAL HADN'T SPOKEN to Faolan since he'd returned from wherever Jonathan had taken him. They'd returned to a world on its head, and Dougal had come back with a renewed sense of purpose. Being the new king's personal guard suited the man. It seemed Jonathan had ensured the man would never be anyone's slave again. In fact, the way he'd grabbed Adair, obviously intent on ripping him limb from limb, was something Faolan had wished to do himself many times. The downside of Jonathan rescuing Dougal was —Dougal ignored him now. Perhaps the man had done so for years, and Faolan had been so busy doing the same, he hadn't noticed. Since the man gave himself up to the demon to save Jonathan, Faolan had seen the truth—he'd failed Dougal. They all had except Jonathan. Their new leader saw everyone's hidden pain. Faolan didn't like it. He kept his shame buried deep for a reason. Now he had thoughts he didn't want. He remembered things he wished he didn't. Dougal caught and held his gaze again and Faolan hated himself for it—like now.

Faolan had been lurking outside the weapons room for fifteen minutes, watching Dougal take apart, clean, and then reassemble every gun they owned. How the man didn't feel Faolan's stare was beyond him. Dougal was shirtless. The Hellish clan kilt wrapped his hips. Dougal was the only one who still owned several. His family sent them to him. Faolan knew Dougal like no one else. He was the only one who cared to noticed Dougal hated pants, and that was the only reason he continued with the plaids.

The muscles in Dougal's back flexed. The muscles in Faolan's stomach tightened. He searched his mind for something to say, coming up blank. Dougal was the only person who'd ever done that to him. Even back when Dougal held his heart, Faolan always found himself tongue tied and never as funny, but Dougal had still always laughed at everything he said. Now he wished he knew what to say.

The hairs stood on the back of Faolan's neck. He spun. The hallway was empty. Faolan narrowed his eyes and searched every dark corner with his gaze. A wisp of something to his left caught his attention. Faolan pulled his knife from his belt before quietly slipping into the dark room. They had several rooms sitting empty on this side of the house. Dougal was the only one who slept near their weapons as if keeping sentry over them. Faolan's senses kicked in, turning the dark room light with his night vision. Another movement out of the corner of his eye had him spinning. A dark plume of smoke, barely shaped like a man, towered over him. Before he could react, his body seized up. He was paralyzed and made mute by some invisible force. In his head, Faolan fought like a warrior while his body did nothing.

"This is for both of us," whispered a familiar-sounding voice before the smoke rushed him and disappeared.

Faolan's knees nearly buckled as he regained control of his body. Except he wasn't controlling his body. It moved without his permission.

Take it like a man.

With Lire inside him, Faolan knew everything. He could feel the demon—knew his thoughts and intentions. He wanted to fight but couldn't while part of him didn't want to fight at all.

That's right, ginger. You know you want this.

Faolan's body ate up the floor—like he had a mission. All Faolan could do was watch it happen through his own eyes. He had no voice or control.

Dougal glanced over his shoulder as Faolan entered the room. "Hey."

"Hey," Lire said without consulting Faolan.

"If you're headed out, I've finished cleaning and reloading that stack there," Dougal said, motioning toward a pile of guns to his right.

Faolan leaned his hip against the table and focused on Dougal. "Nah. Just came to chat with you."

Dougal flashed him a wicked smile. Faolan went

still inside, incapable of fighting Lire's hold. Dougal hadn't smiled at him like that in ages. "Why? Is your jaw in need of exercise?"

Faolan's lips pulled at the corners. Even though he couldn't control his muscles, he still felt everything. "It's been a long time since you gave my mouth a good workout."

A loud laugh sounded through the room. Faolan was a prisoner to Lire and Dougal's laughter. He stared at Dougal's smile. His hunger mixed with Lire's. "What's gotten into you tonight?"

"A bit of the devil, I suppose," Lire said, using Faolan's mouth while Faolan mentally rolled his eyes. "Actually," he added before Dougal could respond. "This is a health check. You need blood."

Dougal's smile fell. "I'm fine."

Faolan moved closer. Dougal didn't move away. "You're not."

"I'm good enough."

"Not if you're protecting our king," Faolan shot back.

"I'll hunt later."

Faolan was dying inside his head. "You'll eat now."

Dougal's throat moved as he visibly swallowed. "Nay," he whispered. "I cannot."

Everything inside Faolan wept as his hand shot out and snagged the back of Dougal's neck. Even if he could've fought, Faolan knew he wouldn't have. Dougal didn't struggle as Faolan hauled him closer. "Aye, you can," Faolan whispered back. He very much feared it had been him and not Lire who'd said the words. Faolan pressed Dougal's face against his throat. He wrapped his free arm around the man's waist, refusing to let him get away. Dougal's lips brushed his pulse. The sensation was so faint, Faolan questioned if it happened. Dougal kissed him again. This time, there was no mistaking the brush of the man's lips against Faolan's throat. "Please?" Faolan begged with a combination of Lire and his desperation. He could feel how Lire had craved Dougal's fangs sinking into his flesh, but he was poison. This was the only way Lire would ever know the ecstasy. Having been beneath Dougal's fangs before, Faolan knew what it was like. He wanted it. "Please?" he begged again.

Dougal's fangs pierced his skin. Lire's moan mixed with Faolan's. Dougal sucked. Pre-cum soaked Faolan's underwear.

I can't touch him with my arms. My touch is poisonous addiction. You have to do it. He needs someone to hold him.

Faolan had this. He didn't need convincing. His dick leaked, and he was half a second away from taking Dougal to the floor. When Dougal licked the wound closed, Faolan struck. He crowded Dougal against the table. The man's hard cock dug into Faolan's hip. His harsh breaths brushed Faolan's skin. Dougal held on to Faolan's shirt as if it was all that kept him from falling.

His gorgeous eyes lifted. Their gazes met. Faolan lowered his head.

"Don't." That one word bounced from the walls and kept Faolan frozen an inch from Dougal's mouth. "Please don't," Dougal said in barely a whisper. "I still want to walk into that fire. Cleaning these guns is the only thing stopping me. Please don't do this to me."

What's he talking about?

Faolan dragged out the memory of Dougal's bonfire, showing it to Lire. Lire's rage filled Faolan's head, turning everything dark.

He released Dougal and took a step back. Dougal's gaze hit the floor. "Thank you for the blood, and…"

Faolan's brain screamed as he realized Lire's intent a half second before the man sprang. His body collided with Dougal's. Their mouths clashed. Dougal didn't fight as Faolan's tongue filled the man's mouth. The brush of tongue on tongue was sweet, making Faolan's eyes burn. It was fast. No more than a taste before Faolan pulled away. He held on to Dougal's head, forcing the man to hold his stare. "If you walk into that fire, I'll fooking kill you myself. I know exactly where you'll be in the next life. That's where I'll find you and kill you again. Your life belongs to me, Dougal."

Dougal's expression transformed from shock to confusion. His gaze moved over Faolan's face. The line between his eyes deepened. "Lire?"

"Say it, Dougal. Swear you won't pull that shit again. You traded your life to me. It's *mine*."

Pain filled Dougal's eyes. "Faolan would hate you using his body to touch me."

Faolan shook his head. "He's along for the ride. You're the only man he's ever loved. He's threatening to unman me for telling you that, but he's cool with me touching you." Faolan shifted closer, letting Dougal feel his arousal. "You're the only one balking."

Dougal closed his eyes as if barely holding his shit together. When they reopened, the man looked more determined than Faolan had seen in ages. "Get out of Faolan's body."

"In a minute." Faolan captured Dougal's lips once more, going deep. Lire's satisfaction combined with Faolan's, scaring the hell out of Faolan. He wanted it. He shouldn't, but the intensity of their combined love for this man was unlike anything he'd ever experienced. This would end. Lire would leave. Things would be awkward. As Faolan pulled away, a shadowy image of Lire still clung to Dougal. Faolan took another step back, watching as the form separated from him.

Lire stared down at Dougal. "Find a way to cope, because I will be back." The shadow disappeared, leaving Dougal and Faolan staring at each other.

Dougal broke first. "I'm sorry."

Oh, good. He'd been right. It was awkward. There

was nothing for it. Some lines couldn't be uncrossed. "I'm not," Faolan said, before turning and walking away. Sometimes there was nothing left to say. Right now, Faolan needed a shower and time to think.

DOUGAL'S CHEST heaved as if he'd been running for miles. His lips tingled. Lire had kissed him and hadn't fucked up Dougal's mind. Lire had kissed him, using Faolan's body. Dear Goddess. On shaky legs, Dougal moved to the door, closed it, and locked it. A lock wouldn't keep anyone out. Dougal needed the illusion.

"On a scale of one to ten, how mad are you?"

Dougal pressed his forehead to the door at the sound of Lire's voice behind him.

It never mattered to life what Dougal didn't think he could deal with. Whatever the worst case scenario was at any given moment, that was what Dougal was handed. He couldn't face Lire yet. "There's no scale. Possessing Faol was the cruelest thing you could've done to me."

"Yet you didn't resist him.," Lire said, close enough to Dougal's ear he could feel the man's breath brushing his neck.

Dougal squeezed his eyes closed and concentrated on the cool wood beneath his forehead. That was real. Lire was smoke and dust with an occasional body. "It seems I'll let anyone touch me," Dougal said, more for himself.

"Funny," Lire said, sounding the opposite. "I wouldn't. In fact, I was very calculating when choosing who would touch you." Somehow, Lire managed to get closer while still not touching him. "Turn around, Dougal. I can smell the lust rolling off your skin. Let me see it in your eyes."

Damn him. Between Faolan's kiss and Lire's proximity, Dougal shook with need. There was no hiding his body's reactions. "Why do you do these things to me?"

Lire's voice dropped to a whisper. "Look at me, and I'll tell you everything."

It was a trap. Dougal knew all Lire's tricks, but he couldn't deny him. With a breath for courage, Dougal turned. Lire's sexy copper gaze traveled down Dougal's body, slowing at his bare chest, before moving to the erection tenting his kilt. When he met Dougal's gaze again, the heat in Lire's stare nearly blasted Dougal off his feet. "You're so goddamn beautiful, and you are mine."

Dougal swallowed. His crown was soaked from the man's presence alone. Arousal sounded in his voice when he spoke. "You said you'd tell me everything."

"I lied."

Dougal's stomach churned. He shouldn't have been surprised, but still. Lire's presence was torture. The demon gave him nothing while expecting everything. "Fook you for that."

One corner of Lire's mouth lifted. "You didn't let me finish. I lied when I told Jonathan I love nothing or no one."

"That's not news. If you didn't love Goddess Celeste, you would've followed in your father's footsteps."

Lire shook his head. "Quit interrupting. It's like you don't want me to tell you I love you."

Lire was right. He didn't, because Lire would never stay with him, and if he did, Dougal would go insane. Having the man's love meant Dougal had lost something special when he'd lost Lire. Something other than his mind.

"I love you."

A gasp ripped from Dougal's throat when Lire said the words. His heart wasn't listening to the thoughts rolling through Dougal's brain. The stupid organ in his chest swelled with pride and ached with loss. Filled with hatred. "What fresh hell are you condemning me to? Do you get off on the idea of me pacing the floors and coming apart at the seams? Do you have any idea how much I want to touch you right now?"

Lire shook his head. "You don't want to touch me. Stroke yourself." The allure in Lire's voice and eyes cast a spell over Dougal—like a cooling balm. His defenses fell. The rage slipped away. Dougal was left staring at the demon who'd stolen his heart. The demon who made him weak and powerful. With one simple tug in the right place, Dougal's heavy kilt fell to the floor. Lire's form solidified. His long curls fell over one shoulder.

"There's a chair in the corner. Go sit in it."

At Lire's command, Dougal turned away and headed for the chair. He kept his movements slow, deliberately teasing. Even when he sat, Dougal slowly slipped lower in the seat, spreading his legs wide and giving Lire a show. Reaching down, Lire stroked his cock through his clothes. Dougal's mouth watered. Lire fed off sex. Without it, he would starve just the same as Dougal would without blood. But the demon didn't necessarily have to participate to feed from the energy. Sex and lust came in many forms. Maybe Lire wouldn't stay, but Dougal would be damned if the demon fed from someone else.

Dougal licked his rapidly drying lips. "Tell me." He knew he didn't need to specify. Lire didn't need urging to make him talk dirty.

"Show me that gorgeous asshole," Lire prompted, and Dougal immediately spread his ass cheeks, giving Lire everything. Lire snapped his fingers. A bottle of lube and a ten-inch dildo appeared on his stomach. "Get to work."

Dougal didn't move right away. "A show for a show."

Lire smirked and unzipped his worn and faded jeans. "Of course. I'm always tit for tat."

When Lire's erection sprang free, his piercing caught the light. Dougal's cock jumped. He lubed the toy before using his fingers and prepping his ass. Ten inches was a lot to take. In fact, it was akin to having his kidneys fucked. There was nothing he wouldn't do for Lire. His fangs cut into his bottom lip as he pushed the dildo past the ring of muscles in his ass. Sweat broke out on his skin as the toy shifted, pressing against something internal and drawing a moan from Dougal.

As Dougal looked on, Lire fisted his cock. Hunger ruled Dougal's mind. He stroked his erection and ate Lire alive with his stare. With his ass full and his lubed fist fucking his dick, Dougal tasted blood as he watched Lire. The man looked every bit the sin he was with his jeans open, copper eyes fixed upon Dougal and jacking off. Pressure beat at his crown already. He wouldn't last long. Lire was too sexual. His demands too hot. He should feel exposed. Instead, he felt powerful. Lire was literally lust on legs. He could have anyone in a glance. Yet he returned to Dougal and claimed his love. Damn, that was powerful. It was intoxicating. This was all he would ever have. It was more than anyone else had offered.

"That's it, sexy. You're almost there. I can feel it. Let it go. I'll come with you." Lire stroked faster as he made the claim. His eyes shone bright and cheeks were flushed. As much as Dougal loved watching that piercing disappear over and over inside Lire's fist, he couldn't look away from his face. Lire's teeth had sharpened. He was full-on demon now. It shouldn't be sexy, but to Dougal, it was all he wanted right now. He gave himself over to the pleasure of his own touch. The sensations and show were too much. Relief poured through him as cum coated his abs and chest. A moan rang through the room. Dougal watched as Lire came. The sight doubled his pleasure.

Lire gasped through his orgasm. "We'll be together, baby. I'll find a way. I swear it."

Dougal believed, and for once in a long time, he was okay. If he never had more than this right here, he'd be fine. Lire loved him. Dougal could feel it. It was more than he'd ever expected from life.

———

HOT WATER STREAMED down Faolan's body, teasing his overly sensitive and long neglected cock. He ignored the sensation as long as he could. Too many things stood in their way. Faolan didn't deserve to touch himself and picture Dougal, but damn. He could still remember the first time they'd kissed. Dougal had ducked into a darkened alcove, hiding from Adair. All the times Faolan had watched the man and dreamed came to a head. Dougal was beautiful. He caught everyone's eye. His long, thick blond hair had the perfect amount of waves to it. Faolan had wrapped that hair around his fist and hung on while Dougal fucked him. Without thought, Faolan lifted his leg and set his knee on the edge of the tub. With his eyes closed and the steam filling the room, Faolan let the sound of the water hitting the tub soothe him. The memory of Dougal filled him. Everyone knew Adair used Dougal every chance he got and pitied him even as they thanked every deity it wasn't them who'd caught the king's eye. Faolan had always expected Dougal to bottom. When he'd taken a chance, he'd been more than a little surprised to find himself sitting on Dougal's cock. Goddamn, he'd been perfect in every way. Faolan fingered his asshole at the memory. Dougal fucked like a god. Faolan had sworn angels sang. He never let Faolan feel like he wasted his time. There was never a ten-second tumble that left him pissed and jacking off. Dougal took his time. He didn't shove his way in and then leave Faolan hanging. Dougal kept him on edge and begging, making him come at just the right moment. Faolan went three fingers deep and tugged at his cock. The image of Dougal, head thrown back and at the edge of orgasm, filled Faolan's mind. That broad chest, straining... fuck. Faolan pumped faster. He rolled his hips, openly fucking his hands. The memory of Dougal melting against him, their tongues brushing as cum filled his ass and the space between them stole its way into his mind. His chest ached even as an orgasm slammed into him, stealing his breath. Faolan tilted his chin back, letting the water hitting his face keep him from screaming his pleasure and chanting Dougal's name. This wasn't enough. He needed Dougal. He wanted him back.

"Goddamn. That was hot."

Faolan scrambled to stay upright as the voice filled the shower. He shook the water from his face. The shadowy figure of Lire stood close enough to get hit by jets of cum if he hadn't been more see-through than not. "What the fook?"

Lire's gaze slid down Faolan's body. "You should get used to me seeing you come. If I'm to be wearing you like a suit, I'll be seeing it quite often. After all, I am a sex demon and I need to feed."

"What the fook?" Faolan repeated because he couldn't stop.

"You heard me," Lire said, smirking. "Dougal traded his life to me for Jonathan's. That's a binding contract. Just because I brought him home doesn't mean he's free for the fucking. If you want that sexy ass, you have to go through me, or rather, let me inside you."

Faolan washed the cum from his hand, giving himself something to do other than look at Lire. First off, he was furious. Secondly, fuck all. He'd forgotten that life trade with Lire. Magical contracts weren't broken. Ever. By anything. Lire could walk away from Dougal. That didn't mean Dougal was free for the taking.

"What do you want?" he asked instead of raging. It wasn't as if he could pretend Dougal didn't matter. Lire had already been inside his head. He knew. Faolan loved Dougal. Always had. He loved him to the point of pain. He tortured himself. Sex with other people, while a necessary evil, had been hell. Every goddamn time, he'd come unglued afterward. That was why it didn't happen often. But with the love was also hate. Dougal was the devil's temptation. He made good men want bad things and Faolan's sister was dead because of it. Lire knew everything.

"I told you. Dougal wants you, therefore I want you. Don't worry. I won't always be around and I'll even let you drive some of the time, but if you want inside my man, you have to take me along."

Faolan grunted, trying to hide the hope tinting his disgust. "And you think Dougal will just go along with the two of us taking over his life? You think he'll let me back into his realm at all? I destroyed him. You had to have seen that while you were poking around inside me. I fooked him up. It's me who made him like that," Faolan said, getting louder with every word.

Lire shook his head—completely calm. "I'm the

one who made him like that, but despite everything, he fell in love with me." Lire took a step closer. Water passed through his body while he still managed to send a spike of fear through Faolan. This demon was full-on badass. Faolan had seen inside him too. He hadn't become Goddess Celeste's private guard by accident. Faolan was good. Lire was better, and he was obviously pissed. "He loves me," Lire repeated. "But he also loves you—always has," Lire said, calming a hair. "You're his kind and his true mate, but I'm his addiction and his life protector. So, where does that leave us?"

Faolan couldn't answer. Lire had called him Dougal's true mate. He'd always known it in his heart. That was why he'd balked at touching anyone else and the real reason he'd gone with Niall when he'd left the clan. He couldn't be away from Dougal. If Adair hadn't given Dougal to Faolan's sister, they'd already be blood mates. They were meant to be—their hearts fated long before they existed. When he didn't answer quickly enough, Lire boxed him against the wall, flattening his palms on either side of Faolan's head. It was odd. Lire didn't take solid form, but Faolan didn't doubt the demon's power to rip him limb from limb just the same. "I'll tell you where that leaves us," Lire spat. "With me wearing you like a fucking suit, driving you like a car, and giving Dougal the goddamn life you've stolen from him for hundreds of years. Understood?"

"I need to think," Faolan said, panic rising in his chest.

Lire's eyes glowed bright. "I'm not asking for permission, so let's play a little game. One where we make a deal."

Faolan stared at Lire in silence. Demons could deal. In fact, they could do whatever for a price. There was only one thing Faolan wanted, or rather, one person. Everyone had taken from the man Faolan loved. One deal, and he could give everything back.

6

The entire house seemed to hold its breath. Between Faolan's kiss the night before and the invitation Jonathan had received from the New Orleans Vampire leadership earlier in the day, everyone was on edge. Jonathan would go, of course. Dougal would be right at his side. All he could do was hope the locals didn't plan to chop off Jonathan's head at first sight. Just in case, Dougal loaded his belt with weapons. He wore his kilt so he could hide as many as possible. They were only minutes away from leaving and Dougal found himself wishing he could steal another moment alone with Faolan. If he died tonight, the awkward way they'd left things the night before would stay that way forever. As if Faolan heard his thoughts, Dougal felt his approach. When the man's fingers brushed through his hair, Dougal fought to keep his eyes open. Faolan tugged as he separated the length of Dougal's hair into three parts and braided them together.

Dougal held still and let it go on. "Who are you today?"

"I'm me," Faolan said in a quiet tone. "I'm always me."

Dougal took a deep breath and jumped in because they couldn't avoid the topic forever. "Last night you weren't."

"Not completely, but I was still me."

Even as Faolan finished braiding his hair, Dougal slipped his gun into his holster. After pulling off a braided leather band from his wrist, Faolan pulled it apart and used one of the pieces to secure Dougal's hair. With his hair out of the way, Faolan's lips touched Dougal's shoulder and lingered. "Stay safe out there tonight."

An unexpected chuckle escaped Dougal. "Jonathan find trouble? Never."

Faolan's laughter caressed Dougal's skin, making butterflies stir in his gut. "Just come home to me."

Dear Goddess, his heart and mind were torn. He didn't know how to respond. Questions rattled through his brain. He didn't have the time or courage to ask. "I'll bring our king home in one piece."

"What's this? Are you worried about me getting

blood on my boots and ruining them before you can steal them?"

At Jonathan's sudden appearance behind them, Faolan didn't move away right away. Instead, he pressed another kiss to Dougal's shoulder, freezing Dougal in place. As far as Faolan knew, Jonathan knew nothing about their past. Yet he didn't seem to care who saw him.

The giant vamp's heat separated from his back, leaving Dougal chilled as he turned to Jonathan. "It's called sharing, my king. I know you're all stingy-like, keeping all your nice clothes, kisses, and computers to yourself." Dougal bit back a laugh at the quick way Faolan said "kisses" as if Jonathan wouldn't catch it hidden in there.

"My clothes wouldn't fit you. You've never used a computer in your life, and my kisses... well, if you want to try it, let's sit down and wait for Niall and Cin."

"I'm in. My only regret is I can only die once for a single kiss."

That made Dougal turn. He had to see Jonathan's reaction. Dougal might've been jealous if he didn't know Faolan. The man was never serious until it came to seduction, then he was focused and deliberate. Jonathan's laughter was worth Dougal's attention. The man had the weight of the world on his shoulders, but he never let them see it.

Instead of buying in to Faolan's ridiculousness, Jonathan settled onto the nearest chair. "We have a minute and we're all friends here who share everything. I've already lost three pairs of boots to you. It's someone else's turn to put out. I'll wait while you kiss Dougal."

Dougal was halfway through strapping a knife to his belt. He went still. His gaze moved over both men. Jonathan smiled like an indulgent parent. Faolan's usual cocky expression slipped away, replaced with a hint of insecurity. He didn't think Dougal would let him kiss him. It was written all over his face. Dougal wouldn't have if not for that look.

Rather than forcing Faolan to battle with his emotions and have someone choose for Dougal... again, Dougal quickly closed the distance between them. He pressed his lips to Faolan's without giving the man time to reject him. He meant to move away as quickly, but he didn't. The instant their lips met, everything inside Dougal lit like a rocket. He didn't forget they had a witness, but he also couldn't move away.

By the time Dougal pulled away, he was breathless. For a moment, they stared at one another in silence before Dougal broke. "I'm sorry."

Faolan's brows drew together. "For what?"

Dougal shrugged. Things were awkward. He felt an overwhelming need to apologize for everything.

Jonathan came to the rescue. "I hate to interrupt

this, but we're running short on time, and I have a serious problem."

He had their attention. They both turned Jonathan's way, but Faolan spoke first. "Lay it on us."

"I don't know what the hell I'm doing," Jonathan said, sounding calm, but the panic was in his eyes. Dougal was a little surprised the man had held himself together this long. "Do I show up there tonight full Nephilim or go as me? If I'm going as Nephilim, I have a clothing issue. Which brings up a whole new set of problems. I've only changed once while wearing anything other than workout shorts, nothing at all, or a sheet, and it didn't go well. Actually, I shredded a t-shirt. It's just a guess, but I'm thinking growing by two feet won't go well in jeans."

It dawned on Dougal that Jonathan wasn't worried about any of the things he'd be worried about in the man's place. Instead of fearing an attack or wondering what his place was in the world, he was having an outfit crisis. The man never ceased to amaze him with his depth of strength.

"You bring up a good point," Faolan said, sounding too serious to be real. "Now I can't stop picturing all the possibilities. What else grows when you get taller? How much more jealous should I be of Niall and Cin?"

Jonathan smirked. An unexpected bark of laughter escaped Dougal. Faolan always met his match when flirting with Jonathan.

"Are we going or what?" Niall said, appearing in the doorway.

"Aye," Faolan said, squaring his shoulders as if he hadn't been drooling over Niall's man.

Niall focused on Jonathan. His features softened. A hot streak of unexpected jealousy shot through Dougal. He wanted what they had. All he'd ever wanted was what they shared. It was always just out of reach. "With luck, we'll be back shortly. Once we scope the place out, Faolan will come back here and ensure the house isn't burned down while Cin and Dougal escort you there. We won't let anything happen to you."

Jonathan flashed a sweet smile. "I'm not worried."

Niall couldn't have looked prouder as he leaned down and captured Jonathan's lips in a quick kiss. "My heart," Niall whispered before Faolan and he disappeared.

The moment they were alone, Dougal and Jonathan glanced each other's way. A silent message passed between them. Their men had just gone into the unknown together. Anything could happen. It didn't matter Faolan didn't really belong to him. Dougal wouldn't survive the loss. The tension was too much. Dougal tried breaking it. "You need a kilt."

"What?" Jonathan asked with laughter lacing his voice.

Dougal nodded, clinging to the topic. "I think a

shirt will be out of the question, but if you wore a kilt, you'd be free to grow."

"Don't get me wrong," Jonathan said, sounding thoughtful. "I think all of this," he said, motioning toward Dougal, "is sexy as fuck in a kilt, but they look complicated and I don't look like you."

To his surprise, Dougal found himself blushing at the compliment. It took him a minute to decide why before he puzzled things out—Jonathan meant it. He wasn't calling Dougal sexy to hit on him or blow smoke up his ass. Jonathan said things with ease that meant everything to others. He was a treasure.

"If you change your mind," Dougal said, trying to stay on topic, "I'd be more than happy to teach you how. It's not that hard. Really, it's just a matter of rolling into it."

The way Jonathan nodded had Dougal believing the man genuinely hung on every word. "Maybe one day when I'm not in danger of doing it wrong and having my clothes fall to the floor in front of a room full of strangers."

"Aye," Dougal said, seeing his point. "Probably best you have a little practice first."

Faolan and Niall reappeared still intact. Dougal released a pent-up breath he hadn't realized he'd been holding. He eyed Faolan, searching for injuries. Faolan winked. Another steady breath filled Dougal's lungs.

Niall had a dark look about him. That detail caught and held Dougal's attention.

"They're in an open and busy area," Niall said, not looking happy about it despite that being good news. "It's a store in the center of all the nightlife here, so they can't do anything without tons of witnesses."

"I sense a 'but.'"

"But," Niall said with a sardonic smile. "We spent a few minutes eavesdropping, and it's obvious they expect Jonathan to be full Nephilim when he arrives. I think anything less will give them the impression he's weak."

Dougal's and Jonathan's gazes met. Dougal nodded toward the door to the weapon's room. His bedroom was across the hall. "Let's go. I'll make sure you're good and tight."

Jonathan stood. Niall eyed them both with suspicion. Jonathan brushed his fingers down the man's arm. "Just give us a minute. I'll proudly go as a gigantic bird. It's not like I'll stand out in the New Orleans party crowd."

Dougal led the way across the hall. The moment they were alone, Jonathan stripped and transformed. Since Dougal knew how private of a person Jonathan was, he did his best to be quick and efficient. Unfortunately, the moment he had Jonathan wrapped in full Hellish clan gear, he found himself staring like the worst of whores. Jonathan looked like a Scottish god. His gold eyes shimmered in the light and he watched Dougal in stoic silence.

Dougal cleared his throat. The words escaped before he could call them back. "Damn, Jonathan. If your men don't fook you tonight after seeing you like this, I'm gonna."

To his surprise, a smile stretched Jonathan's lips. He sat and laced up his work boots as he responded. "I take that as the highest of compliments. Now I get to walk through New Orleans as a gigantic shirtless bird in a kilt. Just like I've always wanted."

Dougal shook his head at Jonathan's dry tone. "No time like the present," Dougal pointed out when Jonathan stood, looking ready to go.

Jonathan followed Dougal from the room. Niall and Cin waited outside, obviously getting stir crazy with the need to get this night over with. Faolan had already disappeared—mostly likely doing his rounds of the perimeter. Dougal bit back a laugh as Cin and Niall caught their first glimpse of Jonathan. He didn't think he'd have to pick up the men's slack when this was over. Dougal hadn't seen the two look hungrier in years.

"Goddamn," Niall breathed.

Cin nodded. "Ditto."

"Let's get this shit show on the road," Dougal said, adding his two cents. He couldn't hang around all this open happiness too much longer. Dougal was one guard for three kings. If he let life kick him in the balls now, he might fail at the only thing he had left— keeping his clan whole.

THERE WAS a real possibility Jonathan might puke. He hoped he did a good job of hiding his nervousness, but seriously. It was bad. Luckily, he didn't stand out at all as they walked down Bourbon. People were packed like smelly sardines and—oddly—Jonathan wasn't the only one with wings. Of course, his were the only ones that were real. Two doors up from their destination, the crowd came to a sudden stop. Someone fingered his feathers. Jonathan glanced over, catching the college-age man rubbing one between his fingers.

Jonathan's nerves got the best of him. He didn't bother hiding his fangs. "It's rude to stroke another man's wings without permission."

The guy immediately dropped his hand. "Sorry, dude."

Dougal's chuckle at his back had Jonathan's irritation slipping away. "Am I allowed to stroke your feathers?"

Before Jonathan could respond, Cin tossed an angry look over his shoulders. "No."

Jonathan bit his bottom lip to keep from laughing. Vampires heard everything. Cin's jealousy was fucking sexy. He lost the battle against the chuckle rising in his throat as he felt Dougal's palm stroke down his wing—openly defying Cin. Jonathan caught the man's eye. "I felt that."

"I knew you would," Dougal said with a wink.

Dougal's smile eased Jonathan's nerves. At least one thing was going right. Maybe it was baby steps, but Dougal seemed to be improving. That thought gave him hope he wouldn't be a complete failure at this huge task that had been thrust upon him.

Outside the door of the voodoo shop, Cin pulled him to a stop. "I know you're silently freaking out," he whispered against Jonathan's ear. "Don't. We've got you, and maybe you're not used to being a king yet, but Niall's been a prince his whole life."

As far as pep talks went, it wasn't over the top, but it went far at soothing Jonathan. "I'm not worried," he lied while keeping his thoughts blocked.

For a moment, Cin eyed his features before giving him a sharp nod. "Here goes nothing." As a group, they filed inside the tiny shop. Everything inside fell silent. All eyes turned Jonathan's way. He didn't smile. His lips being firmly sealed was the only thing keeping him from throwing up.

There were only four men present. Two were identical in every way, down to their hairstyle. Their dark hair and blue eye combination most likely made it easy for them to capture any prey without too much mind control. The man behind the counter was the leader of this band. Jonathan could feel his power. He was old. His dark-blond closely trimmed beard and short cropped hair didn't show a single hint of gray, but he was much older than anyone else in the room. The fourth man clung to the shadows and kept his gaze averted.

"Are you a Scot?" the blond asked, surprising Jonathan with his deep Cajun accent.

"I'm American." Jonathan thought it over, and added, "By birth." His clan moved in tighter. He could feel their collective pride, and Jonathan couldn't stop himself from taking it a step further. "I'm a Scot by the grace of Goddess Celeste."

A round of "Aye" went up around him, making Jonathan smile and the Cajuns laugh.

"Are we meant to bow and scrape to you now?" the man in the shadows asked. His voice reminded Jonathan of a pirate.

"Maybe later," Jonathan answered, since he had no idea.

"You've got yourself two mates, I see," the blond pointed out.

Jonathan nodded. He'd yet to figure out how other vampires knew who was mated to whom.

"That's good. A blessing meant for only the strongest vampires. That's real good," Blondy said. Jonathan fought the urge to shift uncomfortably beneath the collective stares. The man motioned toward the door. "Evan, go turn that lock and flip the sign to closed." One of the twins nodded before doing as told. The blond focused on him once more. "I'm Baptiste. These two," he said, motioning between the twins, "are Ethan and Evan. That one in the corner is Dante." Jonathan nodded at each. "We're your welcome committee. The real crowd is out back. We figured you'd come prepared for an attack, and a smaller group might be best at first. Being as how you're Celeste's blood, we have no desire to end up like Adair. You have nothing to fear from us, but we'd like to know if you intend to screw up what already works or help us clean up the messes that don't."

Jonathan didn't know if he'd walk out back and find himself dead. He had no reason to believe Baptiste. If this man was the leader, as Jonathan suspected, he'd want reassurances. All Jonathan had was honesty. "I'm as surprised to find myself king as you are to have me. Goddess Celeste doesn't make mistakes. You've existed a long time without me. I imagine you'll exist a long time if I'm gone. The only reason I came to New Orleans at all is because we're hunting Mammon."

"Mammon," Baptiste said, scratching his beard. "He doesn't come here. This is the Big Easy. A poor man's resting place. Mammon likes to be where the money is—where greed lives. Las Vegas. New York. That's where you'll find him."

I've been getting hang-up calls from a New York area code.

Coincidence?

Jonathan thought over Niall's mental question. *I don't know. I don't guess Mammon would call.*

"Thanks for the tip. I'm ready to meet your family," Jonathan said, nodding toward the back door. "I can feel their curiosity rising. They're likely to storm the door any second."

Dante snorted. "You can feel them?" His question dripped with condescension.

Jonathan focused on the man. He didn't hold back, giving in to all his power. Judging by Dante's expression, Jonathan looked every bit the Nephilim he was at the moment. "I feel everything and everyone. You're scared I'll find out your secrets. No one in my clan cares you have a werewolf lover." He headed for the back door without waiting for an invitation. The power pulsing through his veins led his action. These men needed to see his strength. He'd show it to them. Jonathan paused beside Dante and met the man's emerald gaze. "I'll keep the rest of your secrets private. Kudos, by the way. I caught a glimpse of your alpha." Dante blushed and Jonathan knew he had the man in his corner. One down, six million to go.

7

A leather braided bracelet sat waiting on Faolan's nightstand. Faolan ran his thumb over the tight design. A smile tugged at his lips. Dougal must have skipped coming through the door and gone straight into hiding. He brought the leather to his nose and inhaled. Damn, he loved that smell. Sometimes he missed the old life—the open sky, heather in the fields, and leather brushing their skin. Faolan recognized what he really missed was the nights he'd spent sleeping under the night sky, wrapped in a plaid with Dougal. They never had much hope of being more than lovers, but there'd been plenty of stars to wish upon.

He wound the bracelet around his wrist and tied the loose ends with his teeth. It had been a damn long time since Dougal had given him anything. Faolan would wear it proudly. After stripping, he sprawled across the bed and stared at the ceiling. He wasn't the least bit tired. His mind wouldn't slow. Probably he should check the perimeter one more time. The last two hundred checks didn't count. Faolan closed his eyes and focused on his surroundings. He could hear every heartbeat. Niall, Jonathan, and Cin were inside their bedroom, speaking in low tones as they whispered their love. Faolan smiled. He didn't want to intrude. Turning elsewhere, he swept the outdoors, catching hints of tiny lives—animals. In his heart, Faolan knew he was avoiding Dougal's side of the house. Faolan was hungry. He should put his clothes back on and go hunt. Before he could stop himself, Faolan's attention swept in Dougal's direction. The man's heart beat fast, as if he was running. Faolan shot from the bed—fear got him moving. He didn't bother with clothes. The idea of getting dressed never occurred to him. Something was wrong with Dougal. There was no time. Rather than race through the house, Faolan concentrated on Dougal's location and dissipated. When his form solidified, Faolan's feet froze to the floor. His tongue stuck to the roof of his mouth. Sweat glistened on Dougal's nude body. The scent of blood coated the air. Dougal had obviously been beating the hell out of wooden fighting posts for a while. His knuckles bled and streaks of blood covered his chest. His eyes looked wild when they landed on

Faolan. It hit him—Dougal wasn't coping as well as he pretended earlier. Without a word, Faolan interceded.

"Is this working for you?"

Dougal sucked in an audible breath. "I can't tell anymore."

With a nod, Faolan closed the distance between them. Dougal didn't argue when Faolan linked fingers with him and headed for the bathroom. "Have you tried relaxing at all? Or is anger your only solution?"

"I don't know how to relax any longer. My mind is too loud."

Dougal's open honesty surprised Faolan. He didn't know why he hadn't expected Dougal to admit to any weakness. "How about I give it a shot?" Dougal didn't respond. Faolan turned and walked backward into the bathroom while holding Dougal's hand. "What do you have to lose by giving me a chance?" Even Faolan didn't know if he meant a chance to help Dougal or another shot at loving him.

Dougal's gaze swept Faolan's nude body. His throat moved as he swallowed before answering. "I have nothing left to lose, period."

It took all his control not to rage against the man's claim. Dougal had him, whether he noticed, cared, or if either of them wanted it. They had each other. Rather than pointing that out, Faolan turned toward the whirlpool tub, stopped the drain, and turned on the water. He tested the temp before adding some bubbles. Faolan moved to the shower and grabbed the body wash and shampoo before coming back to the tub. He set the items on the edge before focusing on Dougal once more. The man's gaze remained locked on Faolan. His skin looked flushed and his erection stood proud. Faolan's stomach cramped with need. He should've fed earlier. The scent of Dougal's blood was killing him. His fangs cut into his bottom lip.

Faolan motioned toward the tub. "Please get in. I have to get that blood washed off before I lose what little control I have left."

Dougal's expression changed from heated to concerned in an instant. "When was the last time you fed?"

"It's been a while," Faolan admitted while confessing nothing. "Please," he added, waving toward the tub once more.

Dougal stepped around him and climbed into the tub. He glanced over his shoulder as he did. "You should join me."

"I intend to," Faolan said as he climbed in behind the man. With Dougal settled between his knees, Faolan snagged the spray nozzle and wet Dougal's hair. He tried being gentle while efficient. Faolan hoped if he made this about taking care of Dougal's physical needs, then he could shield his heart. He swiped his fingers through Dougal's hair, gently working any knots loose before lathering in shampoo. Dougal sat quietly. Trails of white bubbles rolled down the muscles in Dougal's back. Faolan's dick strained to get closer. This wasn't about sex. He refused to let this moment get out of hand. Dougal needed comfort and peace. Faolan felt anything but peaceful.

"Do you remember the loch?"

An unexpected chuckle rose in Faolan's throat. "Jesus, that water was cold. My cock crawled so far inside me every time we got in that water, I don't know how you ever found it."

"We've become spoiled, I think," Dougal said, sounding absent rather than laughing as Faolan hoped. "The creatures of the world have either gotten verra good at hiding their kills or humans are killing each other so brutally we can't tell if we're needed any longer. Either way, we rarely catch wind of anything that needs our attention any longer. Other than a pack of demons floating in the ocean under a shield we can't detect, there's not much we can do but wait to see what'll happen next."

With Dougal's hair clean, Faolan caught himself gently stroking the man's back as he listened. "Everyone was thrilled to meet Jonathan tonight. It seems the vampire community here has been seeking leadership for a while. Only one or two vampires seemed less than thrilled, but that quickly passed when they realized Jonathan is Celeste's great-grandson. In fact, several people offered their lives to serve him. A Nephilim Vampire King is an unexpected blessing to a place that's been without leadership for too long."

"Sounds like you had a very political night. I'm glad I missed it."

Dougal glanced over his shoulder and met Faolan's gaze. "I thought I'd crawl out of my skin before we made it back. Jonathan was so uncomfortable, I thought he might crack. Niall and Cin were cagey as hell. This isn't our life. Our life is a plaid beneath the stars. Not a house with a four-car garage and guardian vamps turning up to serve."

"Is there an in between?" Faolan asked, trying to lighten the mood. "I'm an old man. My balls can't take the cold loch again. Although," Faolan added, touching his lips to Dougal's shoulder, "you were always worth it, even when we did nothing more than kiss." He thought about it for a moment. "Maybe even especially then." Faolan's voice turned thoughtful. They'd spent so long not talking to each other, he had too much to say. "I always hoped—if I made people laugh—they wouldn't notice how unhappy I was."

"Aye. I know."

Faolan tightened his hold on Dougal. "I know you do. You've always been the only person who sees me for who I am. You're so goddamn beautiful—always have been." Faolan thought it over for not the first time. "I suppose that's probably been more of a curse to you than a blessing, but since the first time I saw you, I couldn't take my eyes off you. You tie my tongue."

"And ruin your life," Dougal said, sounding sad.

"Nay. I made my choices. Unhappiness is like that. It eats away at whatever strength you think you have, so when you find something that makes you happy, you don't have the fortitude to resist. There was nothing Adair could've done to keep me away. When Niall made the decision to leave, I could've stayed behind. Cin and you were his strongest warriors. I was just the clown, but even furious and sick with guilt and mourning, I couldn't let you leave without me." Faolan couldn't stop pressing his lips to Dougal's shoulder. "Maybe it was your looks that caught my eye, but it was your beautiful heart that wouldn't let me go."

Dougal drew his knees up and wrapped his arms around them. "It's okay for you to hate me still. Rose would still be alive if not for me."

"Nay. Adair killed my sister as sure as if he'd carried her into that fire. All three of us were victims to our circumstances. It matters not anyhow. I'm still sick with loving you and I won't stop. Not because of our past or because you belong to Lire. I see things verra clear. I will love you always."

Dougal shifted positions, facing Faolan. Faolan held his breath. Dougal's expression was closed. In a move too fast for a human's eye, Dougal slapped his hand down on the button, starting the jets in the tub at the same time as he grabbed Faolan's leg and pulled him beneath the water. The move shocked him enough to have him sucking in a lungful of water. He resurfaced sputtering and coughing. Dougal's head was thrown back. Guffaws of laughter reverberated off the walls of the bathroom. Bucketfuls of water splashed over the edge of the tub as Faolan snagged Dougal around the waist and hauled the man across his lap. As Dougal straddled his hips, the humor drained from his face. His expression turned heated with his gaze locked on Faolan's mouth. Faolan's fingers found Dougal's jaw. He dragged Dougal's bottom lip down with his thumb, determined to taste it. The flavor of the man's tongue lived inside Faolan's memories. There wasn't a detail about Dougal he didn't recall with more clarity than his date of birth. Dougal's heartbeat sounded loud to Faolan's ears.

A loud siren cut through the air, signaling a breach of the property line. Neither of them hesitated jumping from the tub, grabbing a gun, and appearing on the lawn. Faolan focused on Jonathan's life force and appeared in front of him, gun drawn. Dougal appeared beside him, mimicking his pose. Shoulder to shoulder, they protected their king. He chanced a quick glance, checking Jonathan for injuries. Jonathan wore only an unbuttoned pair of jeans. His wings were unfurled and his eyes glowed gold. Reassured, Faolan focused on their intruder.

A familiar face eyed each of them. No doubt they made a hell of a sight. Cin, Dougal, and he were all completely nude while Jonathan and Niall were barely clothed. The intruder's light gray gaze shone heavy with laughter. "Och, did I get here just in time for the annual orgy?"

Jonathan snorted.

Niall shoved his gun in the back of his jeans and stepped forward smiling. "Lachlan," he said with outstretched arms. They hugged like two gigantic bears bent on breaking each other. "What brings you our way?"

"I've come to meet my new brother-in-law," Lachlan said, clinging to Niall as they faced Jonathan. Dougal didn't move aside or lower his weapon even as Faolan lowered his. Jonathan was Dougal's responsibility. Faolan got it, but the man seemed more intense than usual. Niall's brother or not, Dougal didn't seem to care.

I think you're cool to stand down. Even as he projected his thoughts Dougal's way, Dougal didn't relax.

We haven't seen Lachlan in centuries. We nay longer know him. Look at Jonathan. He is still full Nephilim. I trust his distrust.

I'm wearing Cin's pants. If I shift back to being me,

they'll fall down. I'm not as comfortable in my nudity as everyone else around here.

Faolan and Dougal glanced at each other and shared a silent laugh between them as Jonathan's thoughts cut through their minds.

"Isn't that right, baby?" Niall asked, bringing them all back to the moment.

Fuck. Jonathan's curse sounded loud as hell in Faolan's mind. *This big fucking circle jerk of thoughts around me made me miss the fucking question.*

Calm down, baby. Niall's thoughts soothed over everyone even though they'd obviously been meant for Jonathan. "Tell Lachlan he's fine to stay with us. He thinks he's intruding."

That's because he is. Look at all of us. We're more naked than not. We were a few less walls shy of an actual orgy. "Of course you're not intruding," Jonathan said at complete odds with his thoughts. Dougal cast another look Faolan's way. They exchanged another private laugh. "It's almost dawn. You should stay with us."

"Nay," Lachlan said, much to everyone's relief. "I left my mate at a nearby hotel while I came to pay my respects. No offense, but we've never met a Nephilim and Celeste did kill my father after meeting you. I wanted to make sure I'd leave here alive before risking bringing my heart with me."

Jonathan stepped around Dougal and Faolan. Cin stayed glued to his mate's back, obviously protecting it.

"You and your mate are welcome here. Adair had committed many crimes over the centuries. His death sentence was on him."

"Aye," Lachlan said, sounding sad. "He'd done many a thing. I'd been forbidden to visit. With your permission, I'd like to start again."

Jonathan shook his head. "You don't need my permission to see your brother. I'm his mate, not his keeper. We are partners."

Lachlan dipped his chin. "I'll return soon, then," Lachlan said, disappearing as quickly as he'd appeared.

Jonathan eyed everyone and shook his head. A low chuckle sounded from the man's chest. "What a sight we are."

"It's like he stirred up a whorehouse," Faolan agreed, incapable of not seeing the humor in the situation.

"Shit," Dougal said, spitting out the curse. "Once Lachlan tells everyone, we'll never stop getting visitors."

There was a shocked second of silence. It was obvious no one expected a joke from Dougal. Then, as one, they all laughed and headed for the house. Faolan glanced around. They looked like a merry lot of fools, coming home from a night of raucous drinking, debauchery, and lost bets. Celeste was right. This was the clan love built. He wouldn't want to be anywhere else.

A RINGING from the bedside table had Jonathan dragging his ass to Niall's side of the bed. "Who the fuck is calling in the middle of the night?"

"It's the middle of the day for everyone else," Cin said, his voice muffled by his pillow.

Jonathan grunted in way of answer. Everyone else needed to get with the program. Niall had decided to go ahead and visit Lachlan at his hotel room, hoping to ease the man's fears without the added pressure of being surrounded by Jonathan, Cin, and Dougal. Faolan had staunchly refused to let Niall go completely alone. That was fine with Jonathan. He'd rather not entertain anyone anyhow, but if Niall hadn't left, Jonathan wouldn't have to answer the fucking phone. He could've had Niall smash it for him.

"Hello?" Even to his ears, Jonathan sounded half asleep and irritated.

"Jonathan, it's Mike."

"Mike? Oh, *Global Daily* Mike. How can I help you?" Jonathan scrubbed his hand over his face, trying to wipe the sleep from his face while puzzling over why his ex-boss slash ex-everything would be calling. Cin's head popped up at the name. Jonathan resisted the temptation to meet his gaze. Cin hated the man.

While jealousy was sexy as hell on Cin, this was unexpected. He'd thought his ex had moved on long ago.

"I know you're working for a huge paper in Paris, and they're probably paying you everything you're worth, but I'm still hoping I can convince you to meet with me."

Paris? What the fuck? He was half asleep and realizing he should've asked Niall what ideas he'd put in people's heads for his absence in New York. "Yeah, loving it here in Paris," Jonathan said with a helpless wave of his hand since he had no clue what else to say. "Why were you hoping to meet?"

At his question, Cin growled and dragged Jonathan back to his side of the bed. Jonathan swallowed back a yelp of surprise. He stared down the line of his body at the light blue eyes he loved as Cin kissed a path down his body while holding his stare.

"It's no secret you were a huge part of this paper. Your articles have been missed. There's no other journalist out there who matches your talent."

"Um. Thanks," Jonathan said, trying to concentrate as Cin licked his crown. *Evil man.* Not once had Mike praised Jonathan when he'd worked for *Global Daily*, especially when they'd been dating.

Just reminding you who owns this body.

"Like I said, I'm sure you're settled in Paris by now."

"Yeah." The word came out sounding way more sexual than he intended as Cin swallowed his cock.

"Still, we miss you here."

"That's a nice thing to say," Jonathan said, not really listening. Cin's mouth was fucking magic. Only minutes earlier, Jonathan had been dead to the world. Now, his dick beat at the back of Cin's throat, and he was already on the edge. He clung to the sheet. His hips lifted. He fucked Cin's mouth without an ounce of shame while biting his bottom lip to keep from crying out.

"I miss you."

Jonathan's mind went blank. "What?"

Cin sucked Jonathan's balls, rolling his tongue across them before kissing Jonathan's inner thigh.

"I miss you. A lot. I think about you—about us—all the time. It's not like I don't know I fucked up when I lost you, but I kind of hoped—"

Cin's fangs pierced Jonathan's skin. Cum coated Jonathan's stomach. "I gotta go," Jonathan gasped out, cutting Mike off and disconnecting their call. He tossed the phone aside and writhed beneath Cin's touch. "Holy fuck," Jonathan groaned as pleasure pulsed through him. "Damn, I love you."

Cin crawled up Jonathan's body, swiping his tongue through Jonathan's cum along the way before settling between Jonathan's thighs. His smile was unrepentant. "I couldn't let you be tempted by Mike's offer."

Jonathan held Cin's stare, incapable of believing his ears. "Nothing in this life or the next could lure me away." He didn't let Cin respond. Instead, he pulled the man's head down for a kiss. The moment their lips met, Mike's call was forgotten. His life before Cin's touch didn't exist. Still, he couldn't let Cin get away with being evil. With a flip and a twist, he had Cin pinned beneath him.

"It's my turn," he said, straddling Cin's hips and kissing the man's chest. "Call out for Niall." Jonathan listened in, ensuring his orders were followed.

Niall.

Is everything okay?

Jonathan almost felt bad at the concern in Niall's voice, but lessons must be taught. "Tell him what I'm doing to you."

Cin visibly swallowed as Jonathan sat back on his heels. Jonathan recognized the exact moment Cin realized he was in trouble. Jonathan's kinky side had come to play. *Everything's fine. Mike called, and now I'm in trouble.*

What the fuck? What did Mike want?

To beg Jonathan back, of course. But I sucked Jonathan's dick while he was on the phone and now Jonathan is oiling up my asshole. Fuck. He's getting out the big toys.

An evil smile pulled at Jonathan's lips as he listened to their conversation.

Holy shit, Niall. The restraints are out.

Let me tell these guys I've got to go.

Jonathan secured Cin's limbs with the leather restraints. They wouldn't hold Cin unless he played along, but Jonathan knew Cin would do whatever Jonathan wanted. Cin sucked in a gasp as Jonathan slid the biggest dildo they owned inside the man's ass.

"You've got this," Jonathan praised as Cin took the whole thing. With Cin impaled, Jonathan dragged his fangs across the man's abs, narrowly avoiding Cin's erection. Cin whimpered. Niall appeared at the edge of the bed. He took one look at the situation, bent, and captured Cin's lips. Jonathan's dick leaked onto the mattress as if Cin hadn't blown his mind only minutes earlier. He loved to watch his men as their tongues entwined. Watching Cin strain against his desire to snap his bindings, while his cock wept, his ass and mouth full, was the sexiest thing Jonathan had ever seen.

Niall straightened and whipped his shirt over his head before meeting Jonathan's stare. "Where do you want me?"

Jonathan's smile was out of his control. His men knew who would make this worthwhile. "Cin's been bad," Jonathan said, trying to cling to a serious tone. "You're about to straddle his head and choke him with your dick so he can't cry for mercy."

"Oh god." Cin's whisper combined with the pre-cum leaking on the man's stomach was only the beginning.

"I'm about to torture the lower half of his body until he can't walk or get hard again for two days."

"Jesus," Cin whimpered, making Jonathan's evil smile turn that much wickeder.

As Niall stripped and climbed onto the bed, assuming his position without question, it struck Jonathan—this was really his life. This wasn't a weekend out of time. It was every night for all eternity. Blood mates never tired of one another. Each time his life had felt lacking over the years—like he was missing something fundamental to his survival—had led him here. Never had he felt the intrusive hand of fate like he did now. These were his men. Nothing could tear this apart.

THE MOMENT DOUGAL'S eyes opened, his gaze landed on two red roses and a note. They rested perfectly on the pillow beside him. Niall had decided to go see his brother and Faolan had refused to let him go alone. He loved that man's suspicious mind. It seemed Niall and Faolan had made it home safely. After coming up onto his elbow, Dougal unfolded the slip of paper.

One from me and one from Lire. You were sleeping peacefully for once. We didn't want to wake you. — Faol

Dougal snuggled back down. While resting his head on his arm, he stared at the flowers. No matter how he tried keeping his mind blank, it wasn't happening. First, Lire had taken over Faolan's body, using the man to steal a kiss while confessing Faolan's love. Now, Faolan was delivering a rose from Lire. The pair were plotting against him. He needed answers. Closing his eyes, he searched the house for Faolan's heartbeat. The sexy vamp was the first place Dougal looked—in his bedroom sleeping.

Dougal slipped from the bed and headed for the bathroom. He tried not to look at the blood-stained fighting posts as he passed. Dougal equally tried not to eye the whirlpool tub as he brushed his teeth. Instead, he stared at his reflection. There were still dark circles under his eyes, even though he'd slept all night. It seemed he hadn't yet recovered from months of starvation and lack of sleep. Despite the blood Faolan had given him the other night, Dougal's stomach still cramped with hunger.

Tearing his thoughts away from the negative, he tried putting himself to rights. His long hair was a knotted mess. He brushed it until it became a wavy but tangle-free mess. Dougal realized something. He was nervous. It was ridiculous, but he couldn't deny the shaking in his stomach. There was nothing for it. He needed to just do it.

Dougal closed his eyes and focused on Faolan

again. This time, he dissipated and appeared next to the man's bed. A smile stretched Dougal's lips at the first sight of him. Sprawled on his back, with his arm slung across his eyes, Faolan was completely nude. Dougal shamelessly ogled Faolan's body. He could've done so the night before, but he hadn't felt free to let his imagination take hold. With no witnesses, Dougal's dick stirred. Faolan was a warrior. His body was huge and hard—cut to perfection. Muscles bulged and rolled beneath his skin, begging for Dougal's touch. The man's cock was massive even while resting. Faolan was a true ginger all over. Dougal wanted to wake him so he could enjoy the man's rare amethyst-colored eyes. Everything about Faolan was amazing.

Dougal thought of the two roses he'd left behind—one from this sexy giant and one from Lire. Faolan had left them both, accepting an inescapable truth. Dougal belonged to Lire. How many men would he meet who would embrace that? Not that Dougal wanted anyone else, but still. This was the one who'd stood beside him through everything life had thrown their way. So far, Faolan didn't show any sign of backing down from this new challenge. Dougal didn't know what he was supposed to do, but he knew what he wanted.

Without letting himself think too much about it, Dougal climbed onto the bed. Faolan didn't stir. Dougal braced his weight on his palms and licked Faolan's thigh, heading north. He didn't close his eyes.

Instead, he stared at Faolan's cock, watching for any reaction. He was so engrossed, Dougal didn't see Faolan's hand move. His fingers buried in Dougal's hair, dragging him higher. A smile tugged at Dougal's lips as he placed light kisses on Faolan's growing erection.

Faolan gasped. The sound tightened Dougal's balls. He allowed Faolan's crown to slip past his lips. Dougal took things slow. His fangs were out and Faolan's heartbeat sounded loud in his ears. He needed to be careful not to hurt Faolan. Faolan's grip on Dougal's hair turned into a loving caress. He massaged Dougal's scalp as Dougal tongued his slit, searching for any hint of male salt. Dougal hadn't touched Faolan sexually in too long to remember. It had been so long, this may as well have been their first time. Turned out, sucking Faolan's dick was like riding a bike. He immediately hopped on and knew the best route to get the quickest results.

Dougal fingered the line between Faolan's balls and asshole as he let the man's cock saw in and out of his mouth. Saliva rolled down Faolan's erection, coating Dougal's fingers. He used the moisture to push his way inside the man's ass. Faolan's hips left the bed. His hold tightened on Dougal's hair.

"Jesus, I've missed you," Faolan gasped, warming Dougal's heart even as his cock begged for attention.

"Too many nights I've fantasized only to wake to empty arms."

Dougal's eyes burned. He knew that feeling well. Too many times he'd fisted his erection with Faolan's name on his lips only to have the echo of the otherwise empty room consume him. No other loneliness matched loving someone who wasn't there. It was an emptiness nothing filled. Goddess Celeste knew Dougal had tried—alcohol, blood, and other men. Nothing eased his loss. Lire had been the first one to make him forget. Now Dougal wanted it all.

He let his hunger grow as he sucked, determined to make Faolan fly. Soon enough, he'd claim his true mate. He'd waited long enough—made enough detours and mistakes. It was time. Dougal fisted Faolan's cock, jacking him off as he nuzzled the man's inner thigh, inhaling his scent. Faolan's heartbeat grew louder until Dougal couldn't hear anything else. Faolan pressed closer, openly begging for the fangs. Dougal bit. The taste of copper coated his tongue as blood filled his mouth. Dougal swallowed, taking Faolan's life-giving force into himself. Hot cum coated his fingers and still Dougal stroked. Faolan's cries filled his ears and Faolan couldn't stop. He was half crazed with the high of Faolan's pleasure. Even as he crawled up the man's body, reality didn't snap back into focus. All he knew was decadence.

Their tongues clashed and Faolan's hold tightened.

All Dougal wanted was more—everything. He stretched and lubed Faolan's asshole using the man's cum. Dougal was beyond thought. He was madness and need. The way Dougal writhed beneath him fed Faolan's craze. Even as the man's ass squeezed Dougal's dick, Dougal didn't calm. His passion had been set free. Faolan was willingly letting Dougal touch him again. He wouldn't slow and give the man time to think. To reject him.

Beneath him, Faolan was every bit as wild. He strained and clawed at Dougal's back as if trying to pull him deeper. Dougal fucked him hard, slamming home with every thrust, needing to leave his mark. There was something just out of reach he needed more than his building orgasm.

Faolan snagged his hair and yanked, exposing Dougal's throat. His amethyst gaze appeared every bit as insane as Dougal felt. Time stopped as Faolan focused on him. Their stares collided. There was never a chance of going back. Faolan drew him closer, moving slow. Their gazes held until the last second. Dougal didn't miss the ecstasy filling Faolan's expression a half second before the sexy vamp's fangs pierced Dougal's throat. Dougal felt something shift in his soul the second their blood mixed—like invisible strings tying them together. An orgasm slammed into Dougal as Faolan sucked deep, taking Dougal's life inside him. Dougal fought for air. No matter how hard he gasped, it wasn't enough. Pleasure rocked him, taking him to the edge of death. Faolan pulled away. Dougal's blood dripped from the corner of his mouth. Their gazes met. Amethyst eyes turned copper before flashing back to purple. Dougal's mind froze.

"You are the greatest love of our lives," Faolan said, sounding almost demonic as two distinct voices left his mouth. They were both there—Lire and Faolan. They had been all along. He'd just given his life to both.

$\mathcal{T}$he doorbell rang. Jonathan trailed through the house as slowly as possible, hoping someone else would answer. It was lazy, he knew. Life had been draining the shit out of him lately and he didn't want to deal with anyone selling him vacuums or religion. When his unwanted visitor didn't give up, Jonathan gave in and answered. For a moment, all Jonathan could do was blink. "Mike. Wow. Um. How'd you find me?"

The sunlight made Mike's blond hair shimmer. His unnaturally white teeth flashed when Mike smiled. "Sources. Investigation. This is what we do." His gaze swept Jonathan's body. "You seem taller." Before Jonathan could respond, Mike eyed his bare chest and added, "Have you been working out? You didn't tell me you'd moved to New Orleans when I called," he tacked on, babbling and showing an unusual nervousness.

Jonathan scrubbed his hand through his hair, no doubt leaving it standing on end as he tried to decide how to handle this. "Um. Yeah. I was kind of in the middle of something when you called."

"Do you plan to invite me in?"

Jonathan rubbed his chest and glanced over his shoulder, debating. "Yeah. Sorry." This was bad. Jonathan took a step back, silently inviting Mike inside.

"I've sent you a few texts," Mike said as he passed.

"Really? I didn't get them."

"That explains a lot."

Since Jonathan didn't know how to respond to that nonsense, he waved Mike toward the couch without comment. "So, what brings you by?" Jonathan asked, claiming the loveseat across from him.

Mike sat. "As I said when I called, we'd love to have you—"

"Hey, sexy," Cin said, appearing in the doorway and cutting off Mike. "Who was at the... oh, hi," Cin said, pulling up short when he caught sight of Mike. He was being civil, but inside Cin's head, he seethed.

Mike's ass had no sooner touched the couch before he shot to his feet again at Cin's arrival. He held his hand out for Cin. "I'm Mike. Jonathan worked for me at *Global Daily.*"

"Ah," Cin said, accepting Mike's handshake.

Jonathan eyed their joined hands, making sure Cin didn't break him. "I remember hearing the name."

"And you are?" Mike asked, still shaking Cin's hand.

"Cinead. Jonathan's husband."

"Husband?" Mike said, stuttering over the word.

"Aye," Cin said before switching his attention Jonathan's way. "Baptiste is expecting Niall and me. Are you okay or do I need to hunt down Dougal?"

"I'm good. Keep me posted on what you learn."

"You got it," Cin said, leaning down and capturing Jonathan's lips with more enthusiasm than usual. Jonathan knew the show was for Mike's benefit. He wasn't insulted. The gesture was appreciated since Jonathan was getting a definite skeevy vibe from Mike. Of course, it could've also been his left-over hatred from his relationship going sour with Mike. Well, actually, Mike was a big fat cheat.

I want to kiss you goodbye too, but meeting two husbands might be too much for Mike's tiny brain. If he gets out of line, kill him.

Jonathan swiped his hand over his mouth, hoping to hide his smile at Niall's thoughts.

I love you too, baby. Be careful.

Instead of reclaiming his seat, Mike hovered. When Cin straightened away, Mike set his hand on Cin's shoulder, stopping him from leaving. He held Jonathan's stare. "You know, Jonathan, for the longest time, I just wanted you gone." Jonathan couldn't help but notice this conversation had taken a shitty turn. "Over the past few months, I've come to realize, you and me together, we could rule the world." Mike smiled and shook his head, looking entirely too pleased with himself. Cin hadn't pulled from Mike's hold, and Jonathan couldn't believe his ears. "Now," Mike continued, "after seeing you with your blood mate, I know exactly how to control you."

Horror crawled over Jonathan as realization set in —Cin wasn't moving away because he couldn't. Jonathan flew to his feet, transforming as he stood. He wasn't quick enough.

"We'll be in touch," Mike said, disappearing into thin air, taking Cin with him.

Mike is Mammon. Even in his head, the words came out in a roar. Niall instantly appeared next to Jonathan. His eyes looked every bit as crazed as Jonathan felt.

"He's gone," Jonathan said, staring at where Cin had been only moments earlier. "I can't feel him. Even when you were with Celeste, I could still sense your life, but I can't feel Cin at all." Jonathan's panic kept rising by the second.

Baptiste and the twins appeared as quickly as Dougal and Faolan. Dante and three more vampires arrived he didn't recognize. Jonathan didn't know how they knew to come, but vampires filled the room in the blink of an eye. He barely noticed. His whole focus remained locked on Cin, and his search for any hint of his blood mate's life force. When Cin's voice finally filled his head, Jonathan sucked in a breath so hard he almost popped a lung.

Mammon says if you hope to ever see me again, you have to wipe New Orleans of Baptiste and his nest.

Are you hurt? Jonathan couldn't give two fucks about Mammon or his demands. All he cared about was Cin's well-being.

No.

Where are you?

I don't know.

Jonathan wanted to scream. *Look around. Tell me what you see.*

Nothing. It's solid darkness. Even my night vision doesn't cut through the inky void of nothingness.

Jonathan's eyes stung, but his resolve set in. *I'll not be killing Baptiste or his people.*

I know.

But I will save you. Because nothing would happen to Cin or Mammon would never see another sunrise.

I know.

Buy me time. Tell Mammon I need time.

He says you have one day.

Jonathan dipped his chin in a sharp nod. *You'll be home before then, or we'll go to the next life together.*

I'll still love you just as much on the other side.

Same here, baby.

Jonathan grabbed Niall's hand as he met Baptiste's

stare. "Mammon's demand is for me to kill you and your entire nest."

Even though Baptiste didn't appear to move, Jonathan felt him tense. "That's an odd request from a man I've never met."

"It's one I have no intention of carrying out," Jonathan said, reassuring the man of his safety. "But we don't have much time. He gave me one day to comply, so we need to start brainstorming." He focused on Niall. "I don't know why he looked like Mike. Maybe check out Mike's apartment in New York? I don't know if he's possessed him or just mimicked him. Either way, it's all we have to go on."

Niall stole a quick kiss. The hard press of lips on lips went a long way toward soothing Jonathan. "We will find him," Niall swore, sounding certain.

Jonathan nodded. Niall disappeared. He met Baptiste's stare once more. "You said Vegas and New York is where I'd find Mammon. Why would he want New Orleans wiped of vampires?"

Baptiste rocked back on his heels, obviously thinking things over. "New Orleans has always been a demon hot bed. There's dark magic here and an endless supply of human souls to steal. Lots of desperation for demons to feast upon. Being as how Mammon is a prince of hell, he's at heart a demon. Maybe he hopes to claim this territory and feed off the demons' greed along with the humans he already feeds on from Vegas and New York. He is greed incarnate, after all. It would make sense he would try to claim more and more territory."

"Plus, there're ports here." Faolan reminded Jonathan of why they'd come to New Orleans in the first place. "A place where even more demons can pour in," Faolan said cryptically. As Jonathan held the man's stare, his eyes flickered from amethyst to copper and back again.

"Excuse me," Jonathan said, grabbing Faolan's arm and pulling him toward the door. "Don't make me say your name, summoning you from a body you'd damn well better have permission to be possessing," Jonathan spat as he tugged Faolan outside and out of earshot. He turned on Faolan. The man's eyes were copper once more. "If you know where my mate is held, Lire, you'd better speak up. No fucking games."

"You know I'll help in every way I can, but not while surrounded by vampires who'll kill Faolan to get to me," Lire said, his voice leaving Faolan's lips.

"Then let's send these vamps on a demon hunt." Jonathan marched back inside with Faolan on his heels. Every eye turned his way as he came through the door. Jonathan didn't hesitate, telling them everything he knew. "We came to New Orleans on a tip from a demon we captured and tortured. He said this place was being used for its ports, by a pack of demons who stick to the seas like pirates. They travel in huge numbers never seen together before. A few smaller boats break from the fleet, dock at different ports, steal as many humans as they can, gather supplies, and then meet back with the larger ships out at sea. They stay hidden beneath a blanket of wards, invisible to anyone hunting them. If we can find one of the smaller boats and hijack them, we can force them to take us to the larger ships. We could destroy the pack." Lots of mumbling went on around Jonathan about how they'd never heard of such a thing, but it was ingenious. Jonathan ignored them. He needed these well-meaning vamps gone so he could get to Cin. "Maybe if we neutralize the reason for Mammon wanting this place, then we can take back the advantage." More likely, this plan would get Cin killed, but he didn't need Baptiste to succeed; he needed the man to go safely away from him so his clan could work toward rescuing Cin. "If you're willing, I'd like to split up, search every dock for one of their smaller vessels. If you find a demon who can lead you back to their fleet, then we'll use them to our advantage. If you find a demon and they can't help us, kill them."

The crowd was fired up and ready to hunt. Several disappeared before Jonathan even finished speaking until only Baptiste remained. He held out his hand for Jonathan to shake. Jonathan didn't hesitate accepting. Baptiste held tight, obviously hoping to reassure Jonathan. "We'll find your man. You have my word."

"Thank you," Jonathan said, sounding as grateful as he felt. He knew they would find Cin because he couldn't live with anything less.

FAOLAN HAD NEVER SEEN Jonathan furious. He was seeing it now. The instant Baptiste disappeared, Jonathan turned on him. "I don't know what you're doing sharing Faolan's body, Lire, but now is not the time to fuck with me. If you know anything about where Cin is, I suggest you spill now. If you think I can't shake you out of Faolan, I can prove to you otherwise."

"Lire is here," Faolan admitted. "But I'm in charge, Jonathan. I see what he sees. Even if this wasn't an emergency, he wouldn't fuck you over. You're his friend."

Jonathan's shoulders fell and his wings wilted. "I'm sorry." He swiped his hand over his face before meeting Faolan's stare once more. "I have to get Cin back."

Faolan nodded his understanding; if anything happened to Dougal, no one would be safe from his wrath. "Lire is powerful, but he's willingly sharing himself with me, just as I'm sharing myself with him. I can see what he knows. Mammon needs this port. The homeless population keeps the demon fleet fed, but

Mammon can't survive in this realm without a few items keeping him alive—the blood of seven virgins and a host body."

"The missing women from Tortola?"

Faolan nodded. "The seven virgins minus a few causalities. Demons aren't the best hosts for keeping such a prize alive with virginity intact."

Jonathan shook his head. "Putting aside my massive curiosity about the demons' ability to find virgins in this day and age, you're saying Mike is a host body? How long has that been going on?"

Faolan shrugged. "Lire doesn't know, so I don't either, but here's the important part. You said you can't feel Cin. Lire says you need to think about why. If you could feel Niall in heaven, what would stop you from feeling Cin on earth?"

Jonathan chewed his bottom lip as he appeared to mull things over. "A shield of some kind, I suppose."

"But it was instant, like Mammon took Cin someplace already shielded from you, rather than creating a shield after he disappeared, right?"

"I suppose," Jonathan said, nodding. "The moment he was gone, I couldn't feel Cin any longer, and he said seeing us together gave him a new plan, so I don't think he intended to kidnap anyone from the jump. That means he took Cin to someplace already warded for another purpose."

Faolan nodded. "We know of one place already

heavily warded. The same place he's keeping his virgins for feeding."

"The fleet?"

"The fleet," Faolan repeated in agreement. "Unfortunately, even Lire doesn't know their exact whereabouts. He's not a part of the pack. Maybe if Baptiste finds a demon. Otherwise..." Faolan shrugged. "I'm out of ideas."

An evil smile stretched Jonathan's lips. Faolan almost took a step back in fear. "I don't need to know where they are, because I know where they aren't. That's all I need."

Before Faolan could respond, Jonathan reached for Dougal's hand. Dougal's evil smile matched Jonathan's, as if he had the man's back in all things. They disappeared. Faolan turned in a circle. A loud curse escaped as the truth hit him. Jonathan had gone to get Cin with no backup other than his personal guard, and without telling Faolan where they were headed. "Goddamn it." Now everyone he loved except Niall was in danger, and he was standing here fucking impotent.

"Mike's apartment is empty," Niall said as he reappeared. He glanced around. "Where the fook is Jonathan?"

"This one knows where we can find the fleet," Baptiste said, reappearing with a demon in tow before Faolan could answer.

Faolan nearly bent at the waist and sucked air in

his relief. He didn't want to be the one who gave Niall the news about Jonathan and Dougal going after Cin, especially since he didn't know where they'd gone. Now, at least, they had a way to follow. One piece of bad news beat two any day of the week. Maybe Niall wouldn't kill him now, and Lire wouldn't snap his mind over Dougal's disappearance. He was freaking out enough on his own without anyone else's panic.

THE INSTANT JONATHAN'S feet touched the floor of the ship, he felt Cin's life force again. The relief outweighed his rage only enough to keep him from setting the ship ablaze. He didn't hesitate moving toward the sound of Cin's heartbeat. The stench was overwhelming. It was death mixed with unwashed bodies.

"Jesus, I'm wishing away my sense of smell. This trip will make everything I eat taste bad for weeks," Dougal said as he protected Jonathan's back. Jonathan was so goddamn mad, he couldn't even respond to Dougal's banter. The dirty steel walls of the ship's depths weren't thick enough to keep him from Cin.

Jonathan seethed with each step. No one touched his mates. Mammon's attempt to rip out Jonathan's heart had been one thing. The greedy prince of hell was incapable of truly harming him. In truth, Jonathan had been so caught up in trying to help Dougal, Lire, and Faolan, he'd been willing to let things go with Mammon. After all, things had been quiet on the Mammon front for months. He'd thought, foolishly it seemed, that Mammon had been bent on keeping him from coming into his powers. Since it was too late for that, he hoped Mammon would move on.

Now, greed had fucked up. He'd taken things too far. If he'd been smart, he would've walked away from Jonathan and kept his plans small. Mammon could've done a lot of tiny things to stay off Jonathan's radar. Any chance of that was over. No one harmed his clan —much less his mate—and walked away. It was possible he couldn't kill greed—not without impacting the world in a major way. But Jonathan could send the fucker back to hell and make him think twice before crossing Jonathan's clan again.

The closer he got to Cin, the thicker the demons got—like several had been assigned to keep watch over Jonathan's mate. None of them mattered. Each one fell to the ground—dead, as if incapable of surviving in Jonathan's presence. He stepped over their bodies. When he reached the hatch leading to the pit Cin had been stuffed into, Mammon appeared in front of him, wearing Mike like a suit, and blocking Jonathan's path.

"You're stronger than I imagined."

Dougal stood back to back with Jonathan, protecting him from anyone who thought to sneak up on him. Jonathan's mouth lifted in one corner. "Your imagination isn't that big. Touching my mate was a huge mistake." Jonathan moved closer, forcing Mammon back.

Save Cin.

Yes, my king.

Dougal's response went far at proving how frightening Jonathan appeared. He didn't care. His fury refused to ebb. In the past year, his throat had been slit, his heart almost ripped out, he'd been nearly drained of blood, grown wings, and gained two feet in height. Jonathan had done all these things with fucking grace and a smile. It was well past time for some fucking anger. His clan was the only thing keeping him sane, and this piece of shit had dared to threaten that. No more playing nice.

"It's only a mistake if you catch me," Mammon taunted.

The rage brewing inside Jonathan somehow found a way to notch up even higher. One second, he watched Mammon from feet away. The next, he stood toe to toe with him. Mike fell to the ground in a heap. Mammon's form became like dust as he attempted to flee. Jonathan's hand shot out, snagging the man's throat before he could escape. His form solidified beneath Jonathan's hold.

"You were saying?"

A demonic-sounding laugh filled the ship, echoing

off the steel walls, making it sound twice as evil. "You haven't learned all my tricks yet," Mammon taunted.

Jonathan felt Niall appear at his back. The anger drained away. His mates were safe. His clan was still complete. Jonathan held Mammon's black gaze and shook his head. "I don't need to learn your tricks. I have my own." As the words left Jonathan's lips, the dust in his hands burst into flames.

Mammon's laughter deepened, even as he burned. "I'll see you again soon, Jonathan."

Ashes floated to the ground, landing next to Mike's unconscious body. Jonathan stared down at the remnants of Mammon. He felt nothing. "Not if I see you first."

Jonathan turned to find all the New Orleans vampires, along with his clan and Niall's brother, on their knees and waiting at his back. His shock ran deep over their show of respect, but nothing mattered more than checking Cin for injuries. Jonathan patted him down. "Are you okay?"

With a chuckle, Cin covered Jonathan's hands with his to stop his panicked motions. "I'm fine, baby. You can stop."

With Cin's shirt wrapped around his fist, Jonathan blindly reached for Niall. Once he held them both, his heart rate finally slowed. He needed a minute before dealing with anything else. He skimmed Niall's mind, seeing how they'd found their way to the fleet.

"Meeting you has been a blessing, Baptiste," Jonathan said while still trying to pull his shit together. Now that his anger had slipped, the fear driving it showed. "I can't thank you enough," he added, holding Niall and Cin tighter. "You can all stand up, by the way. I don't actually know how that works." A few chuckles sounded as the crowded interior came to its feet.

Baptiste held his stare. "I've no doubt you would've come to our aid too, if the shoe'd been on the other foot."

"Yes, in a heartbeat, but that doesn't lessen my gratitude. What happened to the demon who led you here?"

Baptiste turned, motioning for someone behind him. Dante shoved a demon forward. He looked young. Maybe no more than seventeen to the human eye. His dark, shaggy hair fell over copper eyes filled with fear. A burst of unexpected pity ran through Jonathan. This one probably had never been given a choice in his life.

Jonathan eyed him, trying to decide how to handle this. "Did Mammon put together this fleet or did he take advantage of what was already available?"

"Took advantage," the demon said, sounding as terrified as he looked.

"What's the purpose of so many of you in one place?"

The demon's body shook, as if he expected to burst

into flames at any moment, going the same as Mammon. "We're hunted on land. There's no such thing as home. So we stick to the water and together. This is our pack—our family."

Jonathan met Faolan's gaze, seeking Lire's guidance. "Truth?"

"Aye."

At Faolan's confirmation, Jonathan met the boy's stare once more. "You're standing amongst my clan— my family. Today was the third time in the past year my family has been attacked by yours."

"Today had nothing to do with us," the demon spat, turning defiant. "Mammon thrust your blood mate upon us. He's our prince. We're not given a choice."

Helpless anger looked the same on every creature. Jonathan recognized it in this one. "I know," Jonathan said, softening his voice. "That's why I plan to show you a kindness your prince never has. We'll leave you here in peace, as long as you'll do the same. You saw what became of everyone who stood in my way. There's nothing stopping me from snapping my fingers and turning this entire fleet to ash. That's exactly what will happen if I'm forced to return here. Go in peace," Jonathan said, touching the demon's forehead. He disappeared. Jonathan focused on Baptiste. "I sent him back to his boat where you found him."

"You should've killed him," Dante said, saying what most were probably thinking.

Jonathan shrugged. "Someone had to be the first to show mercy. Maybe it'll matter. Maybe it won't. Either way, thank you for showing up."

Dante laughed. "Not that you needed me."

A genuine smile pulled at Jonathan's lips. "Maybe next time. Let's get the hell out of this stinking place. Jesus, it's like we landed in Hell's bathroom."

As the vampires thinned, disappearing, Jonathan held tighter to his mates. He'd talked a good game, he hoped, but the shaking in his gut hadn't subsided. Next time, he might not get so lucky. They needed a vacation.

9

Faolan took Mike home and wiped his memories. He stopped off at Baptiste's Voodoo Shoppe, dropping off a bottle of whiskey as a way of thanks from Niall before heading home. Instead of going inside, where his mate waited, Faolan walked the perimeter, making sure everything was quiet. He also needed time to clear his head. Their world had exploded before their day began, ensuring there'd be no awkward morning. For Faolan, his dreams had come true the moment he sank his fangs in Dougal's neck. He wasn't as sure Dougal felt the same. The man's expression the moment he realized he'd mated himself to Faolan, with a visitor on board, said a million things and none of them were good. He knew he was stalling against the inevitable. Dougal was his mate now. Faolan couldn't avoid him forever, nor did he want to. Already there was an ache in his gut. Sometimes, Faolan wondered who was the biggest addict—Dougal, Lire, or him.

It's definitely me. Lire's dry tone inside his head made Faolan smile. *I'm just the only one around here who doesn't have any scruples, and therefore nothing holding me back from taking what I want.*

Before he made it to the back door, Dougal appeared from the shadows. "Are you tired of hiding from me yet?"

Faolan's stomach cramped with want. "Aye." Even to his ears, Faolan sounded breathless and aroused. He urged Dougal back into the shadows and against the side of the house.

Dougal didn't argue against Faolan's manhandling. "Why are you avoiding me? Are you regretting me already?"

Faolan traced Dougal's jaw with his fingertips before dragging Dougal's bottom lip down with his thumb. His gaze stayed locked on Dougal's mouth. The memory of waking up with those sexy lips wrapped around his cock wouldn't leave his head. "I love you," Faolan said rather than responding to Dougal's ridiculous question. His only regret was not claiming Dougal sooner. This man had always belonged to him —blood exchange or not.

"I love you too. Don't change the subject."

After dragging his gaze from Dougal's mouth, he

met the man's stare. "That is the subject. I've come to realize there's no low I won't stoop to when it comes to you. There was never a chance of me regretting you. I was worried you felt tricked. Not to mention, I needed a little time to calm down after you disappeared from me today. I didn't trust myself. Lire is demanding blood over that. He's telling me to turn you over my knee."

Dougal's mouth lifted in one corner. His arms encircled Faolan's neck. The space between them disappeared as he drew Faolan closer. "Is that why your thoughts are closed to me?"

"I'm pretty fucking furious with you over scaring me," Faolan admitted. He worked Dougal's plaid loose. "It's a clear night. Lots of stars."

"It is a gorgeous night. I'm Jonathan's personal guard. Not to mention, I'm now a demon's mate. He wasn't getting through the fleet's wards without me." It seemed Dougal wouldn't let this go, even though Faolan had already stolen his clothes. With Dougal's kilt draped over his forearm, he massaged Dougal's cock, hoping to distract him.

"I'll always support your position with Jonathan. He needs you, but don't you ever close your mind to me the way you did today, leaving me with no way to find you. Don't think I don't know it was a purposeful act to keep me from harm. It's been a long time since I made love to you under the stars."

Dougal's hands slid down Faolan's chest. "I feel

both heartbeats inside you." Dougal whispered the words as if scared to voice what they knew was the truth.

Faolan covered Dougal's hands, holding them against his chest. "I regret nothing. I've loved you from the first moment I saw you." Dougal couldn't keep the resolve from his voice. With every word he spoke, his intensity rose. For too long, he'd been forced to silently love Dougal, torturing himself with the man's absence from his life. He'd purposely kept Dougal at arm's length while dying inside without him. His deal with Lire had freed him of all that. Turning away, he spread Dougal's plaid out beneath a nearby tree and sat. He waited. It wasn't easy. Dougal looked damn hot, leaning against the house—naked. Because Dougal still hadn't moved, Faolan took off his shirt.

Tell him to come here or I will come after him.

Faolan refused to let Lire have his way. *He should get to choose. No one lets him choose.* After wadding up his shirt, Faolan sprawled out and shoved the shirt beneath his head. The sky looked endless.

"Hey," Faolan said when Dougal still didn't move. "What's bright and shiny and if it falls out of the sky, it'll kill you?"

"What?" Dougal asked, sounding closer.

Faolan tilted his chin down, meeting Dougal's gaze. "A new car."

Dougal snorted. "You have the worst jokes."

"Maybe," Faolan said with a shrug. "Do I have you?"

Faolan's heart swelled as Dougal dropped to his knees before snuggling in beside him. When Dougal's head came to rest on his chest, Faolan closed his arms around him and held him tight.

"Aye. You've got me." Faolan swore even his heart smiled as Dougal kissed his chest. "You realize just about anything falling out of the sky would kill a human?"

"Jokes aren't supposed to be logical."

Dougal snorted. "They're also supposed to be funny, but here we are."

"Ouch. You're a cruel man. I'll have you know, most people think I'm hilarious. Of course, I had to go and fall in love with the one person who just thinks I'm an idiot."

"You're my idiot."

Faolan rolled, pinning Dougal beneath him. "That I am. Damn, I'm a lucky man," Faolan said more for himself as he touched his lips to Dougal's.

"So you finally got your shit together and claimed Dougal as your mate. Looks like you're not as big of an idiot as you pretend to be."

Dougal laughed against Faolan's lips at Niall's words. Faolan didn't move, even when Jonathan spread a large blanket out beside them. Mostly because he'd stolen Dougal's clothes, and he didn't want to share his mate's sexy body at the moment. Cin, Niall, and Jonathan joined them under the stars.

Faolan turned his head and eyed his friends. "What brings you guys out here?"

Jonathan looked over and met Faolan's gaze. Even in the dark, the man's iridescent eyes—one gold and one green—shined brighter than the stars. They also shone with laughter. Faolan's heart swelled with pride. He had his mate and a new king—one worthy of the position. He'd never known a life like the future he saw before him in that moment. Then, Jonathan opened his mouth and stole his position as the clan's fool.

"I thought it was time for the annual orgy."

Charity Parkerson is an award winning and multi-published author with several companies. Born with no filter from her brain to her mouth, she decided to take this odd quirk and insert it in her characters.

ABOUT THE AUTHOR

*2015 Readers' Favorite Award Winner
*Winner of 2, 2014 Readers' Favorite Awards
*2015 Passionate Plume Award Finalist
*2013 Readers' Favorite Award Winner
*2013 Reviewers' Choice Award Winner
*2012 ARRA Finalist for Favorite Paranormal Romance
*Five-time winner of The Mistress of the Darkpath

Connect with her online:

--Join my street team: facebook.com/TeamCharityParkerson
--Sign up for my newsletter: http://bit.ly/CharityNews
--Website: charityparkerson.com
--Facebook: facebook.com/authorCharityParkerson

facebook.com/TheMenofSin

--Twitter: twitter.com/CharityParkerso

www.charityparkerson.com

admin@charityparkerson.com